Cabbage

Little Kit's
Epic Third Investigation

By
Little Kit

Dedication

This odd tale is dedicated to the memory of both my amazing and wonderful parents and all of their forbears, a handful of whom are included in this particular story.

Foreword

The starting point of this book tells us:-
"Little Kit was jolly surprised to find the small bright red head of John the Baptist in and old wooden box hidden among a pile of forsaken debris amongst all the other stored belongings located in his garden shed in Cardiff."

What follows is the investigation Little Kit undertakes to discover how and why this particular relic ended up in this unexpected location. If this is the sort of thing that might interest you then you might want to read on. If this does not seem to be your "cup of tea" then it is probably wise to give up reading this book now. Little Kit would not wish you to invest any more of your time on something you would not enjoy. After all, there are lots and lots of very good alternatives. His particular favourite author was Jane Austen and so he recommends her, however he understands that everyone has very different tastes in such matters and so would not be the one to overly press his views. He likes to be polite.

If you have not yet read "Camouflage: Little Kit's Epic Mewsings" which was the first book that Little Kit wrote or even his second attempted masterpiece "Subterfuge" then you really should. They go some way to explaining how a very ordinary man called Dave was gradually possessed by the spirit of a small black and white cat. His personal preference in respect of attempted authorship was his first attempt; he had found the second one somewhat less joyous and far more ponderous. In this third book we discover some more about how things in his world seemingly changed from the mundane to the profound and why it is that not all cabbages are quite as 'cabbage-like' as they might otherwise seem.

This particular investigation begins when Little Kit makes an unexpected discovery among all the detritus of his life that has been piled in a neglected corner of the shed at the bottom of his garden. As with all the tales that Little Kit relates the entire framework exists in a universe where absolutely nothing at all is what it seems. You need to comprehend that the gradual onset of vascular dementia overrides everything and so any level of normality is dissolved as the paths of logic are strangled by unintended misdirection and irrelevance.

In his confused and odd way Little Kit seeks to consider the great questions of life. You know the sort of thing: where we come from; why we are here and where are we going. Kit firmly believes that he is a "messenger" but feels that people will only benefit from the information he has to give if they work out the answers for themselves. Basically he really is not the sort of cat who would want to push his own beliefs down someone else's throat. He is much too polite to ever be one of those horrid cats! Kit knows that he is not clever enough to tell you the answers.

From time to time he gets a bit confused, but that is fine, it is all part of the ride we are collectively taking. Due to its disjointed nature as much as the content it covers Kit likes to warn any potential readers in advance that this is not a particularly easy journey an it honestly might not be worth the effort of reading.

Preface

Well what is the difference between a forward and a preface? Little Kit would say that the answer is that he really does not care! You are reading a book being written by a cat and English is not his first language. He would probably not criticise you on your limitations if you happened to write a story in the language that cats have historically tended to use. Now this is important because if these things are important to you then this little investigation is not really the sort of thing you should start to read. Let's face facts; it is pretty remarkable that any book at all could be written by a small black and white cat of unexceptional talent who has taken possession of the mind of a frail, blind old man with organic brain disease. What are you expecting for goodness sake: Shakespeare?

There is an unwritten covenant between any author and any reader that whatever is written should attempt to inform or entertain or evoke a response from the recipient. However, Little Kit is just an analogy for a particular form of madness and really does not care about your particular sensitivities and requirements in this specific matter. It is not that he is being unkind or deliberately seeking to sabotage normal conventions it is just an inevitable by-product of the condition that is affecting him. That said; he strives to be as polite as he can for he does not like rudeness.

He would like you to understand the day to day reality of the madness that envelopes him yet knows that you cannot. Let's face it, even he does not remotely understand it and he is living through it in every moment. Kit knows that no-one ever really understands much about anyone else. Indeed, Little Kit would suggest that everyone actually knows very little about anything at all. We live in a world where all sorts of people seem to think that they know things about all different matters whilst there is no evidence at all for any such boastfulness.

Kit sees himself as quite a simple sort of cat and views the man whose soul and body that he has now possessed that was formerly called Dave as being a particularly ordinary sort of person. He would imagine that you are an equally average sort of person too. He would attribute this to the fundamental nature of the concept of normality verses extremity.

Little Kit would like to give you some idea about what this investigation finds to whet your appetite for the story. So it is essentially about matters of connection. There is a thing called the water cycle when a cloud that is formed by water is happily floating across the sky, then something happens and rain falls to Earth, then it hangs around for awhile and other things happen and then it may or may not end up as a cloud again. It is a fairly simple sort of concept don't you think, all nice and neat which a nice little diagram can show. Now what if that raindrop had some kind of conscious awareness, would that change anything? What is it didn't want to leave the cloud at all, or didn't want to return to the sky at some unspecified point in the future? These are thoughts that bothered Kit.

Then we come to the question of transference. When two objects collide some elements of each moving object are transferred into the other, even at the most minute level. So when a raindrop falls to earth some of the water takes on some bit of whatever it is it has fallen onto and the recipient of the raindrop takes on a certain number of atoms from the raindrop. So it is that if you should happen to kiss someone there is a chance that you might get some kind of something transferred over from whatever it is that has received this particular form of interaction. It is the very nature of things and how the universe whirls around. No one, except Kit, would suggest that a little bit of Judas joined Jesus in that fatal kiss in Gethsemane. However, people might like to think that a little bit of Jesus was absorbed by Judas at some point before he elected to hang himself. So people can sometimes view these things with a specific worldview that influences their feelings on such matters.

What about boxers you ask? When they hit each other do they exchange tiny bits of themselves, do they become a tiny, weenie little part boxing glove now that such things are used, and do the gloves absorb any part of the boxers they have been smashed into. The question of living verses inanimate is quite a tricky old conundrum for a cat to contemplate but he gives it a good old try.

These connections are a matter of particular interest to Little Kit as are the related emotions that all movement engenders. He sees such matters as elemental and likes to explore these in his own peculiar manner. In doing this he really does not care if the reader likes or dislikes what he does or why he does it.

All madness is selfish and destructive. It is terrible to its core. So do not be surprised if a journey into this particular world evokes some kind of negative reaction that is just what it has to do. Everything is a victim of its own nature. So if you had found a small old wooden box in your shed and opened it to discover the shrunken bright red head of a long deceased prophet then you surely would have wondered how it had got there. Perhaps we are al not so very different after all?

The most import thing to remember is that absolutely everything is a message and you only really need to know how to read it. Little Kit always holds to the maxim that if at first you don't understand something then it means you just need to dig just a little but deeper.

1. Consider Parsnips and Cabbages

Cabbage fact: Although it is among the oldest of vegetables scientists have proclaimed that cabbages have only existed on Earth for just about one thousand years. This says something about cabbages, something about scientists and something about us all!

Little Kit was jolly surprised to find the small bright red head of John the Baptist in and old wooden box hidden among a pile of forsaken debris amongst all the other stored belongings located in his garden shed in Cardiff. This certainly was not the most respectable or suitable resting place for such a venerated holy relic. However, even at this very early stage we are getting ahead of ourselves; perhaps we should start this tale somewhere else.

From the outset there a couple of things you should know. At the time we join in his journey in the summertime of the year most British humans chose to call 2019. Little Kit is residing in a small terraced house in an unpleasant suburb of Cardiff in South Wales. As a cat he has a daily routine of wondering around the garden a few times each day, but spends most of his time curled up warmly on a bed firmly engrossed by thinking about his preferred cat based preoccupations. It was always nice for him when he got around to thinking about kippers, but that seemed to happen less and less nowadays.

One of the most important things that you need to know about Little Kit is this: Kit was in fact an ancient spirit that has lived throughout most of history. Throughout those vibrations that you will call time he has mainly occupied the souls of others. Kit the cat has the ability to astral travel through the entirety of time and space and he loves to try and solve mysteries. He has died millions of times and returned in thousands of other forms. At this point Little Kit currently possesses the soul of the man who owns the house. Now the author understands that it might become a little bit confusing for the reader. Particularly in those times when the cat inhabits and takes control of the mentally unwell man that inevitably has also to be called Kit. You might also like to know that the cat has had a nemesis called Pugnance who is featured later in this particular telling of events. So as long as you hold all of this in mind we can proceed with this particular account of events.

In the time before he was possessed by a small black and white cat the man called Kit who was about to enter into madness had a reasonable sort of job. He worked as a manager of a home for disturbed adults who had been removed on a temporary basis from mainstream society to overcome their problems. It was the main function in his role as a manager to try and make those he had been given responsibility to care could become reasonably fit to return to the wider society. Of course, this one sentence alone throws up a lot of questions about the nature of normality and conformity and all that sort of thing, but we are not going to rush down that particular road just yet. We are going to look at a very specific situation.

In his youth the man who became Kit had travelled quite extensively and had visited many of the places that are noted in this particular adventure. It is something of a shame that his mind is now virtually empty and he cannot recall anything about them or what he might have done. Nowadays he simply sits in an armchair with his mouth fallen wide open while gazing into empty space with a hollow stare in his eyes. He had been informed some time ago that it is likely that the vascular dementia he developed will cause him to die by choking himself to death. Inevitably as similar days went by this information dissipated into the wider universe along with everything else that he knew.

Until fairly recently he might have responded to music but that has ended and it seems as if he cannot see nor hear nor understand anything at all anymore. There was a time when he used to repeat key sentences, but even this has now dried up and he does not say anything. So Kit the man that was just sits and stares and waits in darkness whilst a small cat is making use of his redundant soul. Kit's carers come in a couple of times a day to prepare meals and to wash him. None of these carers are aware that he is now possessed by a the spirit of a small black and white cat called Little Kit who has lived many lives and considers himself as something of a detective.

Once again we are rushing ahead of ourselves as the starting point of this tale comes from a period a few years earlier, somewhere around 2010 or thereabouts. The man called Kit was not yet fully possessed by the spirit of a cat and was not even called Kit. In those days before the waiting had begun he had become convinced that everyone on the planet actually saw the world in different ways. To him it was important that the people that he was charged to try and help to progress to conform better with norms discovered this fact too. He reasoned that if they understood this simple concept it might assist them in understanding why their various devious behaviours were so often misinterpreted.

He devised a very simple experiment to help demonstrate the point. There was a daily group each morning in the house he managed and all those living there had to attend. One particular morning he placed a fresh green cabbage on the table in front of those poor souls assembled in their shared mystery and asked them to write three things about what confronted them:

1. To simply describe what they saw on the table?
2. How did they feel about what was on the table?
3. What would they like to do with the object on the table?

It goes without saying that he unconsciously suspected that everyone in the group would say something like they could see a green leafy vegetable, that they did not feel anything in particular about the object and that they would like to put it back in the place where cabbages are kept or perhaps might even want to cook it. Of course, that is exactly what he felt about the cabbage. However it was not the response he got from those in the group. Not one single person said that they saw a vegetable, not one single person mentioned the words leafy or green. So he was pleased that this first part of the experiment rather proved his point and yet was a tad annoyed that none of them got even this most simple exercise right!

Then it got a bit more disturbing. It was very clear that those present in this group did not view the cabbage in a friendly light. Almost everyone responded that they felt threatened by the cabbage and that it held some sinister purpose that was intent on harming them, He had not expected that.

The responses to the third question were even more alarming. Those present wanted to smash the cabbage into pieces or to use it to poison family members. It was clear that he was going to have his work cut out!

Anyway, the underlying point in recalling this incident at this time is to emphasis the underlying principle that none of us actually views anything in exactly the same way. In fact, if you think about it, it is surprising that anyone should ever think that we ever would. We all prefer some songs more than others; we all prefer different shows and hold different political allegiances and standpoints. We all will have different favourite places and could argue about who the best proponent ever was in the history of whatever our favourite sport might be, On reflection, it was a very naive and foolish notion to even begin to think that people might all agree that the key aspect of a cabbage were that it was a green, leafy vegetable.

So we come to the matter of evolution. It is quite easy to see how the biblical tradition of God forging the world and all its fauna and flora that had been believed unquestioningly for thousands of years could have found the scientific challenge presented by Darwin and his like so threatening. It was easy to see how the enlightened folk of the day have embraced this theory and taken it on board with the same level of ferocious zeal as their religious forbearers. Yet Little Kit remains strangely not convinced, For example, he does not see how snakes can suddenly develop poison inside themselves from nothing. It does not take much to question any great theory. Not that long ago no-one knew about dinosaurs and now people have found thousands and everyone believes in them. Not long ago everyone beloved in demons and the reality of Hell; now it is not quite so fashionable,

The timing of this revelation is moot. This came at the point when the mind of the man had just started to come under the influence of the cat that was starting to possess him. He could have easily have carried on believing in evolution with unquestioning obedience like most other humans in the society he lived in. Now he was at the start of seeing things through another's eyes; in particular seeing the world through the eyes of a cat. This might have been the first time he came across the notion of the "universal brainwashing" that became increasingly evident as his possession progressed.

It was not long ago that no one had a computer, or electricity or a mobile phone, well that is the orthodox view of things anyway. To suggest anything otherwise is heresy and madness and utter nonsense, we all know that, don't we?

In another group he asked those present where the best place on Earth they had ever been was. All but two said a local beauty spot, in Mumbles so there unanimity surprised him. One said the cells of a small police station in a nearby village. The most disturbed of them said that he liked Wako in Texas where he had visited the site of a massacre as part of a vacation of pilgrimage to support his religious beliefs.

There was clearly a long path ahead for the recovery process for his clients, as there is for all of us. If cabbage is supposed to be green how come some cabbage is purple? Then what about red cabbage? He had some knowledge of the philosophy of Karl Popper and his sweet little black swan theory looking at the evolution of knowledge. It all sounded so very plausible at the time. Perhaps that is the point?

There are issues of identity and self awareness and potential prejudice that will certainly underpin your considerations. This is not really a problem for most people; they just get on with their day to day life having other things to worry about. In fact, when he was just a normal sort of man before the arrival of vascular dementia and the possession by a small cat it would not have been a subject matter that Kit would have been much bothered with. However, when you wake up every morning and look in a mirror through blind eyes and see a stranger looking blindly back at you then your perceptions of many things change. When someone asks you a simple question like "What is your name?" and you reply "A big red tower surrounded by weeds" then you have an idea that something is off kilter. Especially if you have no point of reference of what the comparative age of a parsnip might be and what this strange point of knowledge might have to do with you.

To people who are not touched by the illness there could be seen to be just mildly amusing. The strange ramblings of the mindless ones can be so unexpected that the only realistic response is to laugh. It is not to be criticised, it is a normal coping strategy that humans have evolved when facing such situations. As his illness developed Kit would realise that he was being absurd and would seem to smile. However the underlying reality is that vascular dementia is just a terrible, terrible thing. As much as people try to make light of it is a long slow death sentence that destroys everything around it.

The human brain is often said to look a bit like a cabbage, but a cabbage is never said to look like a brain. At some point you will find out that Little Kit is rather suspicious of those things that most people would describe as coincidence. In his mind everything is connected and whilst there is always a possibility that some things are connected by random factors he suspects that this is much rarer than you might comprehend. Yet the trouble with being possessed is that the lines between what are the actual thoughts of the host human and what are those of the spirit of a small black and white cat who is an ancient soul that is residing in the soul and mind of the man can become a bit blurred.

2. Consider Pharouk "the Souk"

Pharouk fact: In the older language of the islanders of Socotra the name Pharouk roughly translates to mean "the one who sees".

This story takes place over a number of locations. Some are exotic and interesting whilst others are a bit more mundane. So we will take ourselves off to somewhere as marvellous as anywhere else on Earth. We are going back in time to the rugged shore of a wonderful and little known island in the Arabian Sea called Socotra. It really does exist and if you have a bit of spare time on your hands and you want to know a bit more about it then Little Kit thinks that you might like spend a bit of time finding out more about a place that has long been called "The Island of Bliss".

Here we find two women sheltering from the gentle wind and oppressive heat. In keeping with the ancient traditions of the island Shebatha the Honourable Mother and Megshaom her very expectant daughter had made their way at the due time to the Cave of Birthing on the north of the island at a place called Haq. All was perfectly in place. Little Kit was expectantly watching in his spirit form as he was a welcome guest visitor in the soul of Shebatha. The word had gone around all the usual channels that the newborn baby was going to be rather special.

As you would expect the air was full of the heavy scent of the essential aromatics. The small fire was lit and gently smoking whilst waiting for the various potent additions to join the heady mix. Shebatha was reasonably hopeful that there would be a divine prophesy made manifest at this birthing. It had been a number of years since the island had rejoiced in a direct message from heaven. She knew better than anyone else that she had been pure of heart and followed all the traditional guidelines of the ancients. She had said all the appropriate prayers and entrustments in preparation for this holy hour. The cave was neither dark nor light. The two women supported each other as Megshaom was placed in the birthing position and they began to sing the hymn of expectancy to the one God. All was exactly as it ought to be. A new life was coming.

The breathing and pushing gradually became more earnest and it was clear that poor Megshaom was beginning to experience the pain that has accompanies the arrival of all new human life. Shebatha took the sacred crystals from her waist-bag and started to sprinkle them on the fire. First there was Frankincense, then the resin of the eerily prehistoric dragon-blood tree. This was followed by the brightly coloured petals of the desert rose, nowadays more commonly known as the bottle tree due to its strangely shaped wide trunks. To prove themselves clever it seems modern day botanists have decided to give the endemic plants of Socotra unnecessarily complicated names such as thamnosma and helichrysum and kalanchoe which no-one will ever use. Locals knew them by simpler terms, goats beard, mountain hearts and flowers of dreaming. Many of the plants found on Socotra are found nowhere else on Earth and, like the Galapagos, there are very specific geological reasons for this. Factors include prevailing winds, designated tides and the movement of the crust of the planet. For those of you who still believe that the world is formed by random events a study of this might cause you to ask deeper questions. Yet that is enough of such ranting! Let's get a bit more focused on the birth of the expected infant.

After a number of weighty pushes eventually an ugly little head made its way from the holy womb into the smoke filled half-light of the cavern. Shebatha the holy grandmother gripped the tiny child and placed him into his the expectant arms that were held out waiting to clutch him to the heart of his mother. It was then the longed for vision occurred. Shebatha's face froze into a frame of pure ecstasy as the images travelled though the smoke and into her lungs and brain. It was holy and it was glorious as the breath of new life began.

In her mind's eye she saw the probable future for this boy. It was quite an alarming vision for a grandmother whose only wish was that the child would be healthy and contented. She saw a seemingly broken little man meeting mighty kings. He had very dark skin and the dirty robes of a man who has travelled far. He was marked by God and had just one piercing eye staring wildly around whilst the other was just a hollow wind that dominated his face. However, each of the kings seemed pleased to see and acted as if they might hold him in a place of honour.

This was quite an unusual vision. Most of the prophecies that were noted on the island related to great fishermen, sometimes wise leaders or occasionally strong hunting animals. To see a small old person in dirty robes being hosted by kings and priests was not something that had been seen before.

After the regulated time they took the infant boy to meet the rest of the clan that were staying nearby in the cave of a million dreams, eagerly awaiting news of their newest addition. It was a time of great joy for all those on the island, and particularly for the two holy women. Little Kit had watched the reunion from his astral plane and wondered just what would happen next.

It was agreed the newborn baby was to be called Pharouk. In the older language of the islanders this roughly translates to mean "the one who sees". As you can guess he was to play a prominent but largely forgotten role in how this particular story develops and just a tiny fraction of his unheralded role in the history of Western religion is revealed to you in this tale.

The island of Socotra is just a brilliant place where even greater forces can be seen to ensure that exactly the right plants were growing in that place, and nowhere else in the world. In a long previous epoch Little Kit had been part of a huge community where each collective was expected to follow a particular banner. The motto of the clan that Little Kit had joined was simply "Dig Deeper".

To fully understand the full value of the islands of Socotra to the world humans would need to have a much greater grasp of tides and winds and the movements of the tectonic plates and the history of sorcery and the emergence of life forms and position in the greater dances above and below. It is not the fault of humans that this is not yet known, the information will be revealed when the time is right, in accordance with the sacred holy principles that encompass us all.

So it was that as a youngster following his spoiling the teen Pharouk left his home island with some traders. He could then be found living in the ports around Aden and travelling around the coast of the Arabian Sea. The people of his small island had no real understanding of the world of commerce. They were a largely nomadic people who had enough locally to meet all their need and had no real interest in the trinkets that were craved by others.

Pharouk was really shocked to discover that the common resins he had made on Socotra were considered as extremely valuable commodities in the neighbouring lands. He was a quiet lad who observed all the financial dealings and trades that were being conducted in all of the towns he visited. Various traders used him as a labourer to help move stock around and because he was reliable and honest he was increasingly given greater responsibility. He was not viewed as a good salesman, no-one ever wanted to talk to him, but he soon made contacts in key areas and started to build a reputation for himself as a man who could be trusted. He not only began to trade with other merchants but found himself delivering goods to the many different temples and shrines across the region. He then began to deal with key palace officials and his circle of notoriety grew ever wider.

As you can imagine the system of transport was always quite limited, most dealings of a distance were covered by donkey or camel or ship. Because of his heritage he particularly specialised in resins and so became the key person to deal with in myrrh and dragon-blood resins and bottle tree and frankincense. However he was always open to expand his growing empire and he was able to offer opportunities for people to import and export all kinds of goods, These included building materials, precious stones, perfumes, edible oils, ivory, tin, copper, precious metals, woollen garments and carpets and cloth, barley, and other grains. There was pottery and tents and exotic foods. Eventually he was able to include mercury and sulphur and quartz and exotic minerals to his list of commodities.

As various sundry Kings and Princes continued to make war on each other they required food for their citizens and copper and metal to manufacture tools and weapons of war. Temples obtained the goods needed to conduct both scared rites and secular commercial operations. Merchants grew wealthy and influential. So it was that priests and kings came to rely heavily on traders. It was all very profitable.

Surprisingly Pharouk was not particularly interested in financial gain. He could never really see the point of acquiring wealth for its own ends. Pharouk was mainly interested in matters of a far more holy nature. Pharouk was interested in those matters we now call alchemy, He was interested in the discovery of hidden powers. He was not interested in turning base metal into gold; however he was interested in trying to discover the "Elixir of Life". He wanted to help his Mother and his grandmother. He wanted cure his own form of illness. This was his obsession.

So it was that he wore his travel worn robes and set up a base in Egypt and travelled all over the lands between the Mediterranean Sea and the Gulf of Arabia and had dealings with many of the most important people of the time. He was neither particularly liked nor feared. To the eyes of the world he was simply a very good and reliable trader and that really was quite enough.

However, it was also a time when it was wise to have good business relations and Pharouk from an early age had joined the trader's guild. It was here that he started to meet more powerful men and it was here that he first learned about the glorious society that had became known as the "Keepers of Aaon's Promise".

Oh yes, at this very early stage in his story Little Kit wants to make sure that you know about the strange phenomenon that is called "glossolalia" which is more commonly known as "speaking in tongues", In more ancient times it was known as talking the language of angels. Now to hear Christians talk nowadays you would think it was something they had invented but is was around long before Jesus popped onto the scene. What is not widely known is that this particular practice was very common among the various secret sects where alchemists congregated. There was no end of strange gibberish and supposed interpretation and endless prophecies. Kit wants to mention this now as he imagines that it will probably become more important later on. You will realise that all the people who lived in the emerging civilizations four thousand years ago really believed that they were talking the language that had been gifted to them by angels. Perhaps this is exactly what happened, you cannot be certain because you were not there. However, in one form or another Little Kit definitely was.

3. Consider Prophesy

Prophesy fact: The bible says that prophesy is one of the gifts of the Holy Spirit. Of course, you have the ability to make predictions so what does that say about you? Perhaps you think that it might say more about the information you have been fed?

So what do you think about all this prophesy and premonition malarkey then? As it happens it has been quite an important element of human endeavour since they first crawled onto the scene. Even now you will find most newspapers around the world will include a horoscope at some point. People nowadays tend to be a bit more sceptical than in previous times. There are sports pundits who make predictions based on superior knowledge or simple hunch, just as there are speculators in the shares market. If you look at the role of the Oracle in ancient Greece or the I-Ching in China or soothsayers in the Roman Empire and all other great civilisations you can easily see that prophesy has consistently been a pretty big deal. If we consider the Old Testament it is full of the ramblings of the prophets, and people tended to take notice of what they had to say.

So then we come to the related matter of dreams and their interpretation/ in modern tomes people are not massively concerned about the dreams of others. Of course Dr Martin Luther King is a possible exception. He was a bundle of molecules that had a very specific dream. Kit wished Martin the best of luck with that particular vision of the future. If Little Kit had a dream he would have wanted it to be about kippers but they were more usually about unending pestilence and an endlessly exploding universe. Anyway, for the purposes of this story we need to focus on one specific dream that took place just over two thousand years ago. There is a reference made to it in the gospels of the Bible but they do not give the name of that particular prophet. For that you need to delve into the vast library of forgotten gospels and Holy books that have been shelved.

You probably know chapter two and verses ten to fifteen of the Gospel of clever old Saint Matthew by heart. For those of you who cannot remember this offers details of the arrival of three wise men that popped over from the East. It says this:-

"When they saw the star, they rejoiced exceedingly with great joy. And going into the house, they saw the child with Mary his mother, and they fell down and

worshiped him. Then, opening their treasures, they offered him gifts, of gold and frankincense and myrrh. And being warned in a dream not to return to Herod, they departed to their own country by another way. Now when they had departed, behold, an angel of the Lord appeared to Joseph in a dream and said, "Rise, take the child and his mother, and flee to Egypt and remain there until I tell you, for Herod is about to search for the child, to destroy him."

Now the person who had this dream was a rather battered trader in dirty robes who was called Pharouk, and he came from a place know then as "Island of Bliss" and more recently as Socotra.

It was Pharouk who had met up with Balthazar, Melchior and Gaspar at the pre-arranged destination where he sold them his wares. At this point in time he was the foremost trader of the entire region who could sell precious metals and resins. In fact, he was one of those people who had hundreds of contacts throughout all of The Levant. It was said that Pharouk the Souk could get you anything you wanted and had a reputation for being reliable and discreet.

Anyway, Pharouk met up with the three Magi in a place called the Valley of Kidron which is located midway betwixt Jerusalem and the Dead Sea, now known as Mar Saba. He then went off to the north to meet another King called Philip to in order to complete another very important commission.

You will notice in this quotation from the Gospel of Matthew that Joseph, the step-father of Jesus, had a chat with an angel who advised him to skedaddle south. Now people do not claim to have conversations with angels quite so much nowadays, or to take their opinions quite so literally. Also, someone chatting with an angel might not assume that there will be further interactions at some future point. However, it seems such things were rather more commonplace and accepted in those days. When did that change?

Now when reading the Biblical account of the arrival of Jesus there is a great emphasis placed on the lineage of Joseph as if it was important to meet the requirement of an ancient prophesy that he is descended directly from the blood line of King David. However, as Joseph was seemingly a step-father that all might seem a tad irrelevant to the more questioning among you.

It is not recorded in this particular version of events but Joseph and Mary and Jesus ended up in an isolated mountain called Gebel Qussqam in Egypt where they were kindly assisted by locals who were interested in the wider world. These unnamed helpers liked to know the details of the journey of the Holy family. Strangers were rare and so they were keen to discover more about their beliefs and stories. All Egyptians had a keen interest in natural sciences and astrology. They were fascinated by alchemy in particular. These secluded people also happened to be very good friends with the wandering trader called Pharouk. This was not mere coincidence, after all this was the hiding place for Joseph, Mary and Jesus that he had recommended to the angel.

According to Coptic records after rushing away from Bethlehem the Holy family began their trek into Egypt at a place called Farma and then went onto Mostorod. It is then said they moved on to Sakha before heading off to Wadi El Natroun. The family in exile then continued on to see the pyramids at Giza by Old Cairo, which in one of those historical points of interests that seem to exist simply to confuse us all in those days was called Babylon, and then up to Maadi. Here they hired a small river sailboat to the prosperous village of Deir El Garnous and then they carried on by foot onto the hills of Gabal Al-Teir.

The main stopping point for the Holy Family was Gebel Qussqam. It is believed that they stayed here for six months and ten days. There is an alter to the Lord located half way up the mountain there, where a cave and a water spring and olive trees allowed shelter until an angel popped up to instruct them to go back again.

Given the nature of pilgrimages you would imagine that there would be lots and lots of believers following this escape trail and getting excited about all the key points where the infant Jesus would have slept. However there are no organised tours and there never has been. Such is the random nature of pilgrimages.

At this point in time that does not happen over at Galilee the strange apprentice prophet that became known as John the Baptist was continuing to develop his skills and discovering it was not such an easy trade to master. Predicting the future is easy, any of us can do that. Yet when you actually think about it becoming a chap who washes people in a river and helps them to receive the gift of the Holy Spirit could not have been as easy a process as it sounds. As his Mother always used to say to his critics, if it was easy to make a living out of being a prophet then everyone would do it.

4. Consider Parasites

Parasite fact: Scientists say there are over two and a half thousand different types of head lice alone. Experience tells us these things do not just happen by chance and that there must be a reason for this. Now why do you think there are quite so many varieties?

Perhaps the most disturbing thing Kit had ever discovered was that ninety percent of the human body is made up of bacteria and other non-human calls. In the time when he was just a man he had tootled around quite happily thinking that he was one hundred percent bona-fide human. It was then made very clear that he was barely ten percent human and that he largely consisted of something else that he knew nothing at all about. This is true for you too,

Instantly he was drawn to consider what was the impact of these non human cells and bacteria? Did they have control of his feelings or emotions or thought process? Were they instrumental in any of the bad things that had happened to him or were they a force for good? Where did they come from and what happened to them when he died? This really did need some very careful consideration indeed. Of course, Little Kit thinks these are questions that you should be asking yourself, but knows that most people are all a bit more bothered about doing whatever it is they do than spending time sitting in some bushes seriously considering matters like this. As people always say but never actually provide a proper explanation for; "life must go on". Perhaps there is a sinister reason why it is you are unable to consider the fact that you are only ten percent human?

You will appreciate that it all became even more complex for Kit the man when the dementia set in and he started to become possessed by a small black and white cat. Did the cat only come to occupy his human cells him or did it come to possess the bacteria and other non-human elements within him too?

Many might think that being gradually possessed by a cat is a totally negative experience, but it really is not. Once you get used to the idea of seeing the world through the eyes of a cat a lot of things are immediately improved. For example cats are all totally self centred and self reliant; not at all bad qualities in the wider scheme of things. Some humans believe in miracles, probably more than generally thought, but it is not a subject that is at the forefront of human interaction in the modern day. Meanwhile cats believe totally in miracles and see every moment of each day as a miracle. Every rain drop, every ray of sunshine, every breath and every thought is a miracle in the eyes of a cat. Routine is everything and comfort. They do not bother themselves with science or politics or history or economics or belongings. Cats just exist in the importance of their own "now-ness".

Cats would not have sold weapons so that one group could fight another group somewhere in the Middle-East. Cats would not have invented mobile phones as they are not very interested in what other cats have to say. It is hard enough just being a cat without bothering about anything else other than things that are their own business. Cats would not have followed dodgy leaders and placed vacuous celebrities on pedestals. Humans might think that some cats are better than others, but that is not how cats see things at all. You will see that all cats spend a lot of time just resting. Perhaps there is something that can be learned from that?

There one thing that cats, along with bacteria and every other living being know for certain; only humans would be stupid enough to invent money. Let's face it, all of the rest of the universe trundles along quite happily in its own peculiar way without having to bring any form of economics into the equation.

So we know that parasites survive by living off other creatures and are generally not well thought of because of this. Of course this is a bit unfair as all things actually live off something else. That is simply the way that the universe works. There is neither a bottom nor a top to the "food chain". When the biggest thing gets eaten it decomposes and can end up being dinner for the smallest thing and so the wild journey just goes around and around forever, forwards and backwards in the merry dance we skip around in. However it is always interesting to see where the moral high ground comes from, Cats do not suffer much from morality, and so they can always give a fair overview of such arrangements. Some creatures actually only survive because of their parasites. In the same way planet Earth only survives because of the other planets shield it from particle bombardment. All of these things can be expanded outward and contracted inward. The parasites that live on parasites have parasite of their own. We exist in an endless fractal.

From this we can easily detect clear evidence for a two-way interaction, and without a great deal of thinking take this to more complex arrangements. We then arrive at the logical realisation that all things are utterly dependent on each other. There may be a disturbance caused by death or birth but essentially the pattern goes on unblinking across the eons that do not actually exist. We will probably come onto that a bit later. The mystery of the Great Cycle will become increasing clear. The worm Ouroboros, the mythical snake that endlessly devours its own tail, is a parasite of itself; we are all parasites of ourselves and of each other. It really is not a bad thing; it is a system of perfect wonderment. Cats will usually purr with joy when they think of it.

Now if you were to ask Little Kit what has favourite parasite would be there is a fair chance that he would reply by naming Cymothoa Exigua. It is, perhaps, not as well known a species as many of its more famous compatriots. It is a strange looking skeletal creature which lives in the warm waters of the Gulf of California. It is more commonly known as the "tongue-eating louse". It currently is the only known parasite that replaces an entire organ of its host. This particular parasitic isopod is fascinating because it seems to act in pairs. They enter a fish through its gills. The female will then attach herself to the tongue of the host fish whilst her male partner will fix himself to the gill arches below. Can you imagine the precision and delicacy of undertaking this practice? How on Earth did these tiny little things learn this skill? It really is a wonderful mystery, unless you happen to be the fish that is being visited by them. So then the female will attack the blood vessels to the tongue of the fish it is living in, causing the entire tongue to fall off. Then it simply attaches itself to the stub that is left and effectively becomes the new tongue of the host fish.

Throughout his many travels Little Kit has a whole bundle of stories that could explain to you why the lot of a parasite is not always a pleasant one.

Anyway, this is one of those distractions that impinge in such a bothersome manner in the story telling of Little Kit. Please do not blame him, the trouble with organic mental disorder means that he sometimes does not always stick to the point, but finds himself getting sidetracked. He hopes that you will not find this too distracting; it is just a quirk that happens every now and then. You will almost certainly understand that being a human who is possessed by the spirit of a small astral travelling black and white cat is a situation that is potentially fraught with all manner of communication difficulties.

Now for this particular story we are not interested in how a combatively large parasite can affect the pray it seeks to live off. Instead this entire book is based on the actions of one tiny little parasite of the Acanthamoeba family which took place in the Arabian Sea over two thousand years ago, We must all live according to our nature, if you believe in predestination or otherwise, a cat must be a cat and a worm must be a worm. This is how the universe we live in is properly ordered whether William Blake likes it or not. So is that the unnamed parasite of the genus Acanthamoeba did what it was his entire species have been created to do. They are noted for being an organism that lives exclusively in the cornea of the eyes of other larger animals. It is a parasite that is carried by water and generally tootles along quite unnoticed by cats and humans alike. However, had this particular single parasite not have attached itself to the eye of this one particular boy then the infection would not have caused him to lose his eye and would almost certainly have continued his life as a simple fisherman, as had largely been expected of him. Instead, his face became contorted, his saddened heart became hardened by the taints of others and he left the comfort of his people in the way that outcast's are unwillingly forced to do. Remember, in those days most tribes would have conventions, and superstitions where a badly disfigured face could often be seen as the child bearing witness to the sins of its parents. It was perceived more a sign of punishment from God rather than a little parasite doing what comes naturally. The condition that occasionally causes blindness is called Acanthamoeba Keratitis and it still exists. It inevitably will continue to do so. Thank goodness we all now live in more accepting times.

However, as a final point on this topic for the moment Little Kit would like to stress the point that it is perhaps interesting to see how the actions of one unknown and invisible parasite have impacted quite so heavily on the development of all of humanity ever since. Perhaps this is not quite as uncommon a matter as you might imagine?

5. Consider Plymouth

Plymouth fact: In 1762 the Plymouth Synagogue was built by the local Jewish community to become the oldest Ashkenazi Synagogue in the English speaking world.

Why oh why would Little Kit want to include a chapter on the city of Plymouth? Well in following the

"Path of Melancholia" on his astral travels he was able to determine that this was the first place in Britain where the box he was following had landed. Also, it happens to be a place where an unknown treasure is hidden in open sight for all who care to see and so us worthy of a mention for this fact alone. As the world spins it just happens that Kit had spent a bit of tome astral travelling to Plymouth in previous investigations. Like most dockyards and ports there had been things that happened that some people found regrettable. Certainly when following the "Path of Vulgarity" there were places by the Hoe that might have caused a cat to blush if only they could. Similarly in following the "Path of Corruption" regular visits to the expected haunts occurred with an increased degree of frequency.

History is riddled with small cases of "if only". After it left Plymouth a ship called The Mayflower sailed into a mighty storm. John Howland, one of the Pilgrim Fathers fell overboard but just about with the last attempt of his wildly flailing hand managed to grab the topsail halyards which gave the crew just enough time to rescue him with a boat hook. Among his many famous descendants are the presidents Franklin D Roosevelt, George H W Bush, and consequentially George W Bush. History is written in fractions.

Until five years ago Kit the man had never really liked Plymouth very much. This was not so much the fault of the town itself but more the capricious circumstances that had led him to be there in the past. For those of you who are not aware of his particular gift, Little Kit is a cat who is able to astral travel in both time and space. This has caused him to have a very interesting existence but this has not been totally free of some levels of consternation.

At the time he had inhabited the soul of quite an infamous Jewish diplomat called Samuel Pallache. In 1614 he had plundered a Portuguese vessel and was returning to The Netherlands when a another mighty storm caused his ship to flounder and he ended up being arrested and taken to the nearest sea port. This was Plymouth. This occurred two years before Pocahontas arrived there and a few years before the Mayflower set sail from there, so they were potentially exciting times for some of the locals.

It was not well documented or even much cared about that those searching the impounded ship had discovered in the Masters belongings a strange old box with a shrunken head hidden inside. It was suspected by the unsophisticated customs officials that this had probably previously belonged as mere booty to some unknown Conquistador. Any closer inspection would have shown that there was no logical way this artefact should have been available to these adventurers due to both geographical and historical reasons.

It seems strange looking back on events that Samuel Pallache was eventually found not guilty because his particulate form of piracy was considered as legal. In another unexpected historical twist we can see that it was the non-Jewish community of Amsterdam who raised the funds to send him home. Little Kit did not really remember those parts as clearly as the earlier days when all the Moors in Fez used to spit in his face. He had been forced to live there after his family had been expelled from Spain. Who would want to remember all the stress of being a hated figure on trail and the endless days waiting in a dingy old cell?

Now Samuel Pallache was a pivotal figure in this search to discover how the box with the shrunken red head of John the Baptist ended up in a shed in a suburb of Cardiff. For the huge amount of evidence arising from the study of the astral "Path of Melancholia" Kit was following it was evident that Samuel had been in possession of the relic throughout all his extensive travels. Aside from all his trickery and cunning it was clear that the term "renaissance man" could have been created with him in mind.

Little Kit would like to tell you a lot more about him because he really did have a very interesting life, but he does not want the story to become too bogged down in details. This was a trap he just seemed to fall into all the time.

So we shall quickly move on to thinking a bit more about the town of Plymouth itself. In far earlier times Little Kit had lived in Oreston cave and that had been quite a miserable sort of existence. There was just too much time spent on surviving and not enough time for leisure pursuits. This was not a particularly uncommon situation in those days.

At that particular time the large ones were still hanging around and an extraordinarily large chap called Gogmagog was particularly loathsome. He used to try and hunt and kill all the local animals for fun. So it was that no-one was particularly sad when he and his kind died away. The caves were a better place to be without them around. Well, that was until the smaller ones arrived anyway.

It is hard for people to understand, but cats see everything as interconnected. To explain this principle in the complex way that cats prefer would be pointless. Perhaps you might need to consider molecular structures to help explain it? Every single thing in the entire universe is totally different and yet collectively works to ensure the whole is fully functioning. This includes every single atom and every micro second of time. To humans who like more simple forms of explanation it is rather like "The Force" in Star Wars, but it does not have good and bad properties. It is beyond mere morality and is all both good and all bad in all places. Space is not upon impinged by immature judgements and labels. It is a principle of completeness that is innately understood by all life forms. It is only humans who have tried to educate themselves away from this who think anything different. Cats find this funny.

Cats are also acutely aware that the human notion of time is deeply flawed. They still seem to think it has some kind of lineal progression. Cats would spend far more time doing things rather than sitting down resting if they shared this concept. No, they believe that all of time is present in the same moment. Each second is precious to a cat because it is the only second and it is also eternity. To a cat it is all very simple, the entirety of us all is simply a cabbage and a cabbage is all we are. Cats do not get vexed on issues around how the cabbage came to be, it is enough for them that it is there. They are not a species who wants to invent problems for themselves, exactly like most of the other species in the universe. For cats, the concept of "now-ness" is quite enough.

Anyway this was not really what Kit wanted to tell you about Plymouth! What he wanted to get across to you were the principles of cluster. Now you will know of all sorts of different places where certain important people have been drawn together either by chance or by design. Little Kit is not a great follower of thoughts around chance and so will usually hold a view that such gatherings are inevitably preordained. So let's think of a few examples to clarify the point. There are all the artists who lived in Paris at the same time, all the famous gothic writers or all those English romantic poets. During the industrial revolution we saw the emergence of new engineers who were perfect for the times they found themselves living in. There have always been inventors but wherever there is a golden age of great inventors they can usually be seen in the close proximity to others who have encouraged or challenged them. There were clusters of builders all at the same time – no one seems to be building stone circles anymore but there was a fairly long period when they were popping up all over the place. So was it one single person or idea that acted as a magnet for other to join them or some other force. Kit was tempted at this point to start thinking about the glory days of Venice, but remembers that he is writing here about Plymouth. It is always to tempting to get enticed down these different pathways!

For the purposes of this tale it is probably sensible to stay in South Devon in and around the time of the sailing of the Mayflower. Plymouth is still quite a long way from anywhere of importance in particular and this was, even more the case in those days before trains and nice comfortable roads. So we see over quite a short period of time Plymouth had all the Pilgrim Fathers various infamous pirates and associated others, Sir Frances Drake, Pocahontas and Samuel Pallache all turn up and play their particular part in world events. Let's face it; Plymouth has got quite a lot to answer for!

Little Kit likes this idea of clusters. For the purposes of lots of his stories he likes to think of Jerusalem. For the bible stories to work out well it needed all sorts of different players to be around at the same time. It might have all been very different if, for example, Judas had been born a hundred years later. For what is called the greatest story ever told it needs Pontius Pilate, Herod the Great, the Magi, Barabbas, John the Baptist, Lazarus, Mary Madelyn and all the other characters, big and small, to be in exactly in the right place at the right time.

In his astral travel following the "Path of Melancholia" that emitted from the old wooden box it was clear that it had arrived from its unexpected sojourn in the Caribbean into Plymouth at some point. Kit was pretty sure that it was brought into Britain for the first time when Samuel Pallache was arrested. The pathway after that was relatively easy to follow, even its strange but eventually false excursion into Burma. However Little Kit had followed these traces for many eons and was only too aware that the pathways of relics were often filled with such surprises.

At this point we essentially wash our hands of Plymouth. It was just a stop-over on a much longer journey. If ever you should visit it has been said that the aquarium there is really rather good, unless you happen to be a fish, which you almost certainly will not be at this particular moment in time.

6. Consider Pugilism

Pugilism fact: The very great boxer Sugar Ray Robinson actually backed out of a boxing match against Jimmy Doyle following a dream that he was going to kill his opponent in the ring. A priest and minister convinced Robinson to fight so he went into the ring.
Sadly Jimmy Doyle was killed.

At this juncture it might seem that the tale he is telling is starting to go off on a tangent here and you might be concerned about this. Certainly it is not a simple progression taking us from near Jerusalem to Cardiff in any sort of simplistic fluid ordination. Yes there are quite a few different individuals who Little Kit wants you to consider before getting back to the Middle East. As with all good investigations there are a whole cast of different suspects. Some will be relevant and key to the centre of the plot and others might be just "bit players" who somehow muscle in on the action with no apparent reason. To understand quite how the box with the shrunken head ended up in his shed Kit had to take quite a lot of different factors into consideration and this is just one example of that process.

Kit had been thinking to himself that perhaps there is an invisible force called "patriotism"? It was just a thought. You are probably not aware or much interested that in the pessimistically named World War One there were many battalions of small people who signed up that were called the Bantam regiments. Any fit young man who was under the height of five foot two inches could have the pleasure of joining the bloodbath. One such soldier was Charles Hiscox. He had already followed another invisible call to leave his pleasant green rural Somerset home in Darshill to join the massed ranks of the industrial revolution digging coal in the horrid grim blackness of Mountain Ash in Glamorgan. He set off to France to do his duty and spent a number of years digging trenches, getting bombed, gassed and shot at whilst coping with lice and trench foot and madness in all its varied forms.

Little did he know when he was sitting in mud getting attacked by complete strangers with all his new short friends around who were similarly being shot at that he would soon return home to a country where his government would try deliberately to starve him into submission? At that point he did not know that he would have a fifth son who he called Douglas. It was this son who would go on to be in procession of a box that held the bright red shrunken head of John the Baptist. If you had told him he really might not have believed you. It really is a strange old existence we lead sometimes, isn't it?

Now in the previous chapter Little Kit introduced you to a few different characters that will be popping in and out of the thread of this story for different reasons as he tries to make sense of the discovery of the box in his shed. He is now about to introduce you to a few more people who might help in considering this fundamental underlying issue of connectivity.

During his extremely varied lifetime of possessions Little Kit had been occupied in the souls of crushing millions, Cats are part of the fabric of all things and are much better connected to this fact than humans, who barely understand the concept. Carl Sagan wrote about a small pale dot and was considered very wise indeed. Cats do not have to write about it. As with much of the rest of this Earth, it just comes naturally.

Kit was using his leisure time to think about four of the boxers that he had been enmeshed with. The first was Daniel Mendoza, the second was Walter Neusel the third was Henry Armstrong and the most recent was Douggie Hiscox. On the face of it there is no particular way that these four men should be connected, and it is initially hard to see how these people across different generations and geographies were aligned, and yet they have been.

So we start with Daniel Mendoza. He was a larger than life street boxer from the East End of London. As it happens, he was a direct descendant of Samuel Pallache. You will understand that such issues arise in many clans and races and religious groups by the way that humans organise themselves by such shared traits. You do not see all the black and white cats of the country hanging around in one corner of Britain refusing to mix with and hating all the ginger cats who live in another part, but humans still have so very, very much further to progress and they are not showing any significant signs of moving any further forward.

We have established that Dan Mendoza was the first champion boxer to feature in this particular trail of events. Little Kit knew that, for some time he had been in possession of the mysterious shrunken head and was curious to investigate how this had come about.

One of the things Kit the cat enjoyed most was looking at the providence for what are called "out-of-place" artefacts as he was very keen for humans to understand that they are living in an entire universe of lies and that it is the discovery of their true history that will allow them to achieve true enlightenment of the utter futility and magnificence they are embroiled in.

Daniel was a famous Jewish prize-fighter who became the boxing champion of England in 1792. His boxing career started in quite a romantic way. When he was sixteen he was working for a tea dealer in Aldgate in East London, He became aware of an incident between his employer a frail gentleman tea dealer and a more robust tea porter who challenged the richer man to a fist fight. As was allowed in those days, the young Daniel Mendoza stood in for his employer and won the bout. This provided him with certain notoriety and he went on to have many brutal fights including defeating the colourfully named Harry the Coal-heaver.

The sport of bare knuckle fist fighting was officially prohibited but we all know that it took place illegally and was very popular. In particular people liked to have a bet on the winner and so it was that a number of fortunes were won and lost on the outcome. It was a pastime that appealed to people across all the usual social divides. The rich and powerful of the land were drawn towards these secretive events and it is noted that Mendoza's fight against Sam Martin in 1787 was arranged by the Prince of Wales himself. Daniel won in ten rounds.

Following the astral travel and simple detective work Little Kit had undertaken it was clear that Daniel from an early age had been in possession of the shrunken head in a box. It had been passed onto him from his Father who had no further use for it and realised that, of all his children, it was Daniel who would probably be able to benefit the most.

Before Daniel Mendoza boxers of the time generally stood still and merely swapped swinging punches. Mendoza's style consisted of more than simply battering opponents; his "scientific style" included much defensive movement. He developed an entirely new style of boxing incorporating defensive strategies, such as what he called "side-stepping", moving around, ducking, blocking, and basically just avoiding punches. It makes so much sense writing about it now, but humans have not always been the brightest of animals. At the time, this type of fighting was revolutionary and Mendoza was able to overcome much heavier opponents as a result of this new style.

Although he was only five foot and seven inches high and weighed just one hundred and sixty pounds Daniel Mendoza became England's sixteenth Heavyweight Champion reigning from 1792 for three years. Yet why stop at England? Daniel became the first middleweight ever in history to win the Heavyweight Championship of the World.

In 1789 he opened his own boxing academy and published one of the earliest books on boxing titled *"The Art of Boxing"* which was a modern approach that every subsequent boxer learned from. It has been suggested that due to his fighting capacities Daniel Mendoza helped transform the popular English stereotype of a Jew from a weak, defenceless person into someone a bit more deserving of respect. It was not a view that Little Kit saw much evidence for himself in his astral travels of that period. Also, English people had to be pretty stupid not to have understood that history was full of examples of battles and bravery akin to all other groupings. However, this is the nature of prejudice discrimination and it will probably always be that way for as long as humans have anything to do with it. It is always wise to try and avoid the punches that are thrown at you.

As this story progresses we will come across a few people who seem to have been able to cross cultural divides. Daniel is said to have been the first Jew to talk to King George the Third. British Royals and next generation Jews just tended to move in quite different circles in those days. The invisible forces of race were an ever present feature of the day, just as they are now. Mendoza acted as second for a freed American slave in his fights. London was a cosmopolitan sort of place and a melting pot where diversity was a largely unrecognised invisible force, as it mostly has been.

It was in Hornchurch in Essex in 1795 that Daniel Mendoza lost his title when he fought for the championship against Gentleman John Jackson who was on his own particular pathway to infamy. Boxing fans might be well aware that Jackson was five years younger, four inches taller, and a hefty forty-two pounds heavier. As you would expect, the bigger man won. It lasted for nine rounds and ended with the "Gentleman" grabbing the long hair that Daniel

Mendoza sported and whilst holding this with one hand simply pounded his head with the mighty fist of his other hand. The battered head of Daniel Mendoza was savagely pummelled in this way for around ten minutes before he was forced to concede defeat.

Daniel proved to be s man of vary many varied talents and used his much battered head to good use for the betterment of his family. Mendoza began to seek other sources of income, becoming the landlord of the "Admiral Nelson" pub in East London. Of course, he did not retire from pugilistic activities altogether. For instance in one of his astral journeys Little Kit saw him slugging away in the March of 1806, Mendoza had returned to prize-fighting and enhanced his already legendary status by defeating a chap called Harry Lee in a bruising fifty-two round encounter. Subsequently Daniel turned down a number of offers for re-matches and in 1807 wrote a letter to *The Times* in which he said he was devoting himself chiefly to teaching the art. However, in 1809 he was hired by a theatre manager in an attempt to suppress some riots but the resulting poor publicity cost Mendoza much of his popular support because he was seen to be fighting on the side of the privileged.

Mendoza made and spent a fortune. His memoirs report that he tried a number of different ventures aside from being a pub landlord and opening his famous boxing academy at the Lyceum in the Strand. He toured the British Isles giving boxing demonstrations; he appeared in a pantomime; he worked as a recruiting sergeant for the army and even had a go at printing his own money. He became what

Little Kit might call a working class "renaissance man".

It was just one day short of his fifty-sixth birthday in 1820 that Dan Mendoza made his last public appearance as a boxer. Banstead Downs had been selected as the venue for a grudge match against nasty Tom Owen and Dan was defeated after twelve rounds. One of the greatest skills a boxer needs to have is to know when to quit.

History has shown us that Daniel Mendoza was considered as intelligent and charismatic but also chaotic. Little Kit has always believed that Dan was clearly drawn by brilliant but invisible unknown forces. He died at the age of seventy-two, leaving his family in poverty. The few possessions he had left simply passed on down through the family. Among them were an n ancient looking wooden box that no-one had ever bothered to open. So no-one ever knew what was inside the box. It is probably just as well, it is not the sort of thing you want sitting in your dining room is it?

Previous to this the last place that Little Kit had located the box was in Amsterdam. The Mendoza family were part of the bloodline of Samuel Pallache and they seem to have brought the relic over with them when it became possible for Jews to live in England. Someone from the family had written a book in English about how to prepare meat using the approved methods of the one true God to his chosen people and it was that which was seen as being the real treasure of the Mendoza family. The box was just something that never managed to get itself thrown out. Little Kit knows that most households have all sorts of strange and obscure items like that. No doubt you will have some too?

So the unappreciated holy relic was just passed on down to various assorted children. This seems to be common practice among Jewish families and is equally true of most refugee communities. Invisible family ties are important. Researchers have shown that Peter Seller, that much heralded and talented was one of Daniel Mendoza's great-great-grandsons and he hung portraits of the boxer in the backgrounds of several of his films. However he was actually quite an unpleasant sort of chap and it was certain that box would not end up with him! One of the men who wrote the well known ditty "Oh I do like to be Beside the Seaside" was another in his ancestral chain who failed to inherit the relic. Oh there are just so many connections that Little Kit can get lost down here. He has to remain focused for you.

As it happens the next place that Little Kit was able to place the old box in with a strong degree of certainty was in the back of a small watchmakers shop in Mare Street in Hackney. Here it had been passed from Judah Aarons who had briefly gone to play music in America before returning to London and going insane. His son Frederick inherited it as another part of all the old tat that the family had gathered around them in their various travels.

Ancestral bloodlines are not as important to cats as they are to humans. They would consider the notion that any particular feline would be considered as superior and even be the king of the species simply because of a result of breeding some three hundred years ago as quite a preposterous idea. It was not that cats are overburdened with heightened concepts of equality. It is just that they are naturally far more rational than those who have adopted an upright nature.

So the trail goes ever onward, both forward and back. Of course Dan Mendoza was a descendent of the useless conquistador, the hated rabbi, Samuel Pallache, His descendants went on to have affairs with Princesses, write the lyrics to popular songs and followed endless other useless paths. One descendant was a man who sold sponges in Petticoat Lane; another was Frederick the clock maker who travelled selling alabaster figures and his family. One of these was his daughter Amelia Aarons who grew up and married Little Douggie Hiscox. This is where our diverse boxers and the old wooden box are strangely connected in the tangles of time.

The second boxer Little Kit discovered had briefly been connected with the shrunken head was the German heavyweight champion Walter Neusel. History shows us that he was known as "The Blond Tiger" and was a very good looking chap. Neusel had turned professional in 1930. He won more than he lost and was rewarded just four years later in Hamburg when he took part in a very important bought facing the great Max Schmeling. The audience figures were said to reach nearly one hundred and twenty thousand people which holds the record for being the largest amount of spectators in German history. On first appearance it seems very unlikely that such a figure would ever get close to a small box being held by a Jewish family now in the south west of England, but that is what happened.

Kit had been able to discover that Little Douggie used to box for the Apollo Club in Torquay and they had invited Walter Neusel to train in their gym. It was probably not a good time for a German to be visiting England but Walter and Douggie got on happily despite the imminent arrival of the Second World War. Walter had actually carried the box when Amelia and Douggie were helping her family to move house across town and that is how he had a faint trace on the "Pathway of Melancholia"

The madness that forms the politics of men rumbles onward. So it was that Douggie Hiscox was sent off to do his duty; just as his Father Charles had done in the previous major conflict. There were all sorts of early diversions but Douggie ended up being shot at and bombed by Japanese people to whom he had never been properly introduced over in the jungles of Burma. It was during this time whilst he was temporarily located down in Calcutta that Douggie got involved in an unexpected event that led Kit to investigate the very limited role of the next boxer on his list.

The American world champion at three different weights was Henry Armstrong. He was on a tour of the troops to help boost morale and it had been arranged for him to fight in an exhibition match. So it was that the totally unknown plucky little Welshman was picked to represent the British Army over there in order to complete a bought with one of the best boxers in history. All this took place in front of 175,000 people at the Electric Cinema. It was a wonderful claim to fame but Douggie never spoke of it afterward. Perhaps we all have interesting stories to tell and yet to us they might seem utterly pointless and not worth mentioning.

So although it was not immediately obvious, the next boxer known to have some connection to the box with the shrunken head, was the American Henry Jackson Junior, He was quite particular about what he was called and mainly boxed under the name of Henry Armstrong, He also managed to acquire nicknames like "Hurricane Henry" and "Homicide Hank". He was also known as Melody Jackson in his early fights, but discovered that no-one was particularly worried about fighting an opponent called Melody! As we progress through this story we discover that names are oddly important. Following his astral travels it became clear to Kit that Henry had never actually touched the box, and may never have even been within thousands of miles of it, and yet he had just the faintest of trails left on the "Pathway of Melancholia". This must have been because of the transfer of molecules, nothing else makes sense!

There is no reason why anyone reading this book should have any particular interest in boxing, in fact it is far more likely that the sensitive folks who are attempting to follow this odd little saga will have an intense dislike of violence in any form. Henry Armstrong was very famous indeed being the first person to have been declared as world champion in three different divisions at the same time; those being featherweight, lightweight and welterweight. Foe many he is considered one of the greatest boxers who ever lived. He actually had a fight to try and gain the world middleweight championship in an attempt to become the first man to hold titles at four different weights, but the bout was called as a draw. In 1945 he retired after 182 professional fights, of which he won 152 with one hundred and one knockouts. That was an excellent record. He went on to be ordained as a church minister and to follow the traditions of John the Baptist until he died in 1988.

Little Kit was wondering what all this had to do with events in Palestine some two thousand years previously and was beginning to think maybe this was one of those intermixable paths he would travel down without any clear connection. Now here we are, this wild prophet of old called John had the same profession, washing random people, so that the Holy Spirit could enter into strangers via water.

This is an altogether mysterious and strange old concept, yet it is a process that is carries on all over the world thousands of times a day. Given that these primeval forces gather together in a world where such matters are not a general subject of conversation is a great peculiarity don't you think? To a conspiracy theorist these things are manna from heaven. In modern times it is increasingly shameful in a secular society to even say the words "Holy Spirit". It is a subject that is not talked about in polite society anymore.

If Little Kit were to ever utter the words "Holy Spirit" in public the people listening to him would automatically consider him as being mad, which of course, in the truly organic sense he actually was, because that is the nature of vascular dementia. Oh dear, we were trundling along quite nicely, and now all this has come along. It is the sort of place where some people might feel their investment into this tale is not

52

worth the effort and will stop reading. Don't worry if you feel the need to leave us here. There are many books that Little Kit had started to read and yet just found himself unable to manage more than a couple of chapters.

So, to continue, the one boxer in this chain that links them all together in the loosest of ways is Little Douggie Hiscox. Of course he ended up with the box before Kit and so we might come onto thinking about him a bit further along as Kit supposes that you will be a little bit fed up just being introduced to dead sportspeople and will want to move on to something a bit more interesting.

All you need to know at this point is that the "Pathway of Melancholia" that Little Kit was using to follow the train of the old wooden box has suggested that Daniel Mendoza had held the box in his pub, The Admiral Nelson at Whitechapel. It indicated that the popular German boxer Walter Neusel had carried the box in South Devon but had probably not actually opened it and had no idea what it contained, It showed that the American Henry Armstrong had also been close to someone who possessed the box when he visited North-eastern India but there was no evidence that he had actually seen or touched the box himself. It was just the way that the merging of lines on an astral path like the "Path of Melancholia" that was being followed by Little Kit can throw up diversions and points of interest.

It seemed very unlikely that a young British soldier like Doug Hiscox would have taken the sacred procession to Burma. So it seems far more likely that it was the spirit within the box that travelled with him whilst the actual relic remained in Torquay before moving on to found by Little Kit in a small shed in Cardiff at a house owned by his blind and deranged son.

It is clear that relics have power. Just because humans do not understand what that power is does not make it any less true. Quite a lot of the writings talking about things that happened in the time we now call history relate to issues around the mastery of power. In fact there are quite a few wars and struggles that are built solely around this matter. Little Kit would have liked to have used this point to speculate some more on his thoughts about this particular issue. You know the sort of thing, what if Germany had developed nuclear weapons first, or the Japanese had used an atom bomb first in America, all that kind of idle speculation amused him. However, reflecting on what might have been is not getting us anywhere nearer to where we are heading is it?

Kit was finding it hard to keep up. This seemed to be an epic tale of conflict and normality over generations. All very "Roots" you might think and cats have a better innate awareness of bloodlines than humans, who are strangely quite backward in these things. Human scientists have only just discovered that over half of all the water that is found on the planet was formed in space before the planet Earth was ever actually formed. Cats are not overly bothered by this type of awareness, however for humans it should be a key to greater level of understanding of the kind most animals and plants already possess. This is real "Roots" for you.

The practical application of the possession of the mind of a human by a cat is something that can happen quite slowly; well it was in the case of Little Kit anyway. At first the man was fearful of the possession and resisted its intrusion. However as he slowly learned that all he had ever been shown as a human was lies and misinformation he started to appreciate the clarity of the mind of a cat and even began to embrace this invasion.

Kit thinks this has been quite a long and difficult chapter to traverse. He hopes that you are starting to understand invisible and difficult concepts of powers we do not yet comprehend and do not even have a name for. He feels that he has tried, perhaps in a clumsy way, to demonstrate that possession can take many thousands of different forms. Surely you must by now realise that you yourself are actually currently possessed by simply thousands of things and that you do not understand any of them. That is all a part of "The Great Lie" that we have all happily signed into.

7. Consider Piracy

Pirate Fact: A Jewish pirate called Abraham Henriques Cohen who had been previously tortured under the Inquisition was responsible for the biggest heist of treasure from the Spanish fleet. In 1628, he captured a fleet conveying gold and silver worth twelve million guilders, around $1 billion today.

Abraham Cohen has nothing at all to do with this tale but Little Kit found the stories of these Jewish pirates interesting. Similarly he found the ones of the female Welsh pirates equally fascinating and thinks the study of these would form the basis of a good discussion around norms and morality for any budding scholar. In essence most people seem to have very interesting lives if only you choose to dig a little bit deeper.

You would think that an eye patch was a fairly straightforward thing for humans to invent. Sadly the concept came a bit too late to help Pharouk who had to bare his terrible and savage scars to anyone who dared to look Yet there are lots of pirates who took full advantage of the added protection a nice little patch could provide, Apparently they were created to help people see in the dark, surely that is why God created carrots?

When you are an ancient soul who has lived millions of lives then you will almost certainly have met lots of people and it is not surprising that Little Kit could not remember everyone's name. This was particularly the case since he contracted vascular dementia which just made everything a bit more "foggy" for him. He had tried his hardest for you but the name of the useless conquistador just would not come to him. If he were a human he might possibly have been able to look it up in some computer search engine, but he was a cat and paws and "qwerty" keyboards are not entirely compatible. Humans have a very strange way of wanting to introduce rules to everything. There are rules for fighting and even rules for piracy.

It seemed like a good idea to the useless conquistador who was the grandson of Geronimo of Valladolid to follow the footsteps of his brothers and sail off to the New World in pursuit of gold and the

"Tree of Life" all for the glory of the Church and Spain and for his very nearly noble family. However, there is always paperwork to consider in these matters and before he left he should have sought the written permission of the King of Spain. This was a pretty significant oversight as a few years later he was not allowed to keep any of the treasures that he plundered.

At this point Little Kit will desist from writing more about the hopeless conquistador who happened to be a direct forbear of Daniel Mendoza. He is a character who loosely pops up elsewhere in this story because it is one of the pillars of connectivity that Kit tends to bang on about. What Little Kit was able to determine from his astral travels along the "Pathway of Melancholia" is that the box that held the head of John the Baptist was carried to the New World and was handled or approached by various men who could be considered as legal pirates. It was difficult to determine the full facts but it was pretty clear that at some point the box was able to infect or have an impact upon both the ineffectual; conquistador and also a very different chap what was called Juan Leon de Ponce, It seems as the relic itself was a force that was driving those it influenced to approach various sources where the "Elixir of Life" could be found. Perhaps the head of John the Baptist was able to influence those around in an attempt to recharge itself with the power of the Holy Spirit? Kit realises that this is a difficult concept to understand. There are millions and millions of forces that underpin human actions that they have simply no grasp of at all. The useless conquistador was eventually promoted to become the Governor of a small island but died within a few months causing the entire area to collapse into riot and chaos. It was clear that he had not found the "Water of Life" that he had been sent out to search for.

Now Little Kit was trying to be clever at this point and had aligned his astral travel following the melancholia of John the Baptist with the seafaring and piracy of the characters included in this tale and their bloodlines. So it was he found himself chasing the information that developed around a ship called the "Penula". It was a half mast and half steam boat that sailed out of Aberaeron in West Wales. Its captain was a female who was the great grandmother of Douglas Hiscox. The ship has sunk in a heavy storm off the coast of Naples. However there is absolutely no record of the boat in any of the usual sources. He was able to discover that her family had originated in Southern Carmarthenshire, but little else other than a link to s mariners training school that had been established by Aberaeron Harbour. It was evident that she had started her carrier by stowing away on her Father's boat as it exchanged trade with Egyptians in Alexandria, but the trail went surprisingly cold in all directs other than a descendant called Margaret Lloyd who ended up in Mountain Ash married to Charles Hiscox, who had come across to join the colliery workers from his family base in Pilton a small hamlet in Somerset. You see there really is a lot of information but the number of pathways and trails just expanded like the family of a single parasite finding itself on a nice healthy food source. Little Kit was finding it very difficult indeed to keep to the point. Vascular dementia not only causes you to forget things, but it also seems to ensure the mind of the one who is being assaulted by the disease just jumbles everything up. He hopes you have patience to stick with him as he works a way through the maze of shadows he encounters.

So what you need to know is that there are legal pirates and there are illegal pirates and their legitimacy seems to depend on whose side you are on in respect of the division of the spoils they obtain. If you are Spanish then you will might Juan Ponce de Leon, if you are Dutch or Moroccan then you might like Samuel Pallache. If you are Welsh you will like your seafaring female captains, Morality balances on the strangest of fulcrums don't you agree?

So we see that there are different types of pirates who seem to be drawn together by invisible forces to create clusters. The Caribbean Sea was a particular magnet for all manner of pirates at a certain point, as was Plymouth at another point in the story. We find Socotra is currently being used as a base for the Somali pirates of today. This might mean nothing at all or this might be a point of significance. These were the kinds of thoughts that wondered through the mind of Little Kit in those moments when he was not dreaming wistfully of potential future kippers.

8. Consider Ponce de Leon

De Ponce Fact: The third largest city in Puerto Rico is called Ponce in honour of the Spanish explorer Juan Ponce de Leon.

Now we come to a strange point in the story where Little Kit had used his astral travels on the "Path of Melancholia" and discovered that the box with the head of John the Baptist had been taken to the Caribbean Sea. It seemed to him quite a strange turn of events altogether,

It was one of those murky pathways where the evidence was hidden. Little Kit became obsessed with an attraction within the Mendoza bloodline to another key figure that could have been called a "renaissance man". This is a Spanish nobleman called Juan Ponce de Leon who was born in 1460 and died sixty-one years later. This was a chap who had all kinds of different claims to fame. He was another who had been very near to the box that held the shrunken head of John the Baptist and perhaps may have actually touched it, but there is no clear evidence of this. However, he was obsessed with finding the "Elixir of Life" and the "Pathway of Melancholia" showed that he was potentially very close to achieving his goal.

As you will have gathered, Little Kit was always very interested in tracing old bloodlines. It might not be of interest to most people but when it comes to looking at the genealogical trail of the Mendoza family he has detected a direct link here which is relevant to the journey of the box that holds the bright red head of John the Baptist.

The surname Ponce de León dates from the early thirteenth century. In 1235 Little Kit had been invited to the wedding of a nice girl called Aldonza Alfonso who was the illegitimate but recognised daughter of Alfonso 1X the King of Leon and a blustery sort of chap who was called Pedro Ponce de Cabrera, He found them a pleasant couple who were perhaps just a bit too pernickety. The descendants of this marriage added the "de León" to their name. So we finally arrive at the birth of Juan Ponce de León in a small village over in the Spanish region of Valladolid.

The reason Little Kit is stressing all this detail is because at some point, after the battles with the Moors, the box with the head of John the Baptist arrived in this area carried by Samuel Pallache before being taken to the sunny Caribbean. Is seemed odd to Little Kit that these people were so closely tied by the Mendoza bloodline and had been seeking out possible previous connections. As much as he tried to follow the trail the exact details were blocked. He found some links to a military force that was called the "Order of Calatrava". Little Kit was also finding out what role they played when the box had ended up with the alchemists of Fez. He suspected this was somehow related to the re-conquest of Spain in 1492 when a rather grumpy chap called Pedro Núñez de Guzmán, became the Knight Commander of the Order of Calatrava at which point Juan Ponce de Leon was his young squire. He knew that he would need to dig a bit deeper if here were to get to the bottom of all this.

Now Juan was thirty-three when he popped over to the New World with Christopher Columbus and that crew. Ten years after he was the Governor of Hispaniola when he decided to explore Puerto Rico in search of gold. This really was something of an obsession for Spanish adventures of the time. There he had been told that the "Fountain of Youth" might be near there on the small island of Bimini. So it was that he set off to bother the people who were living there. Now this is a difficult place for Little Kit to be because he really wants to explain to you about the ancient buildings in the sea there, but he is determined to be disciplined and assumes that if you are keen on these matters you can look it up for yourself.

Following his role in crushing the Taino people of Hispaniola and stealing their mines and farms and then starting plantations his arguments with Diego Columbus, the son of his former boss, got worse. Taking the advice of the King our chap Juan then set off on the first Spanish expedition into Florida. It wall went quite well for the Spanish and in 1513 Juan Ponce de Leon returned back home to his family home It was a memorable visit for him as he was knighted by King Ferdinand. He was a determined sort of fellow and decided to go back to Florida to see if he could find the "Fountain of Youth" hiding over there. As it happens Juan was certainly not the last person to do so.

As you might have expected, the local Caluse people really did not want a colony of Spaniards on their land. It was perhaps a pity that he did not share your level of insight into such matters. One of them shot an arrow coated with the poisonous sap of the manchineel tree into Juan. As intended, this caused him to become very ill indeed and his men took him back to Cuba where he died soon after. Little Kit reflected that history is full of these sorts of skirmishes and they never seem to end well.

There are lots and lots of labels that you might want to give this man. A number of these might alter across time as sensitivities are readjusted. Was he a hero, a politician, a military commander or a pirate or profiteer? Was he a noble pilgrim hoping to spread the word of his mother church or perhaps he was a tyrant or a fool? He was certainly an explorer and is nowadays thought of as a conquistador. Anyway, it all sounds like he had a jolly interesting life and now there are a number of big statues dotted around the region so that people can remember him and honour him should they wish to do so.

Well Little Kit knows that there is a lot more you probably want to know about this man. It is clear that he had a jolly interesting time all things considered. He was another of those people who ended up dying simply because of the arrival of a very tiny substance into his bloodstream. He will not be the only mighty one to be laid low by something that is deemed vastly inferior. Little Kit is always keen to remind people that even Alexander the Great who was considered by many as the greatest man of the period on the planet died as the result of an infection carried by a mosquito. The inference of this is almost Biblical in its proportions. The very smallest of things can influence the entire planet. Why can humans not see this?

9. Consider Perspective

Perspective Fact: There are various perspectives on what a perspective might be depending on your starting point. It could be a visual issue presenting the way something appears or the effect it engenders. Or it can be the context for beliefs, experiences and opinions. Sometimes it might even suggest the vantage point itself.

"She has the morals of an alley cat" is a fairly well known old saying. Perhaps it is a tiny bit misogynistic: but we have already discovered that many things are coloured by the mores of the time as they come into and out of fashion. Perhaps the world does not always spin at the same pace for everyone? Anyway, the point is that cats are considered to be a tad loose in the department of moral probity. This is quite true, cats really do not care if something is good or bad, they are accepting and intelligent animals who do not use crude terms of judgement and feel a much better because of it.

So it was that when the mind of Kit the man became possessed by that of Little Kit the cat he actually started to feel a great sense of freedom. It did not matter that poor people are exploited and that there is no such thing as justice in the universe. Things simply are!

You do not see cats waging silly old wars just because some other cats are living on land where oil deposits can be found. Quite frankly they would much rather simply sniff each other's bottoms whilst leaving all that other stuff about ownership to a more stupid group of animals who have not yet grasped the reality of their limited position in the greater scheme of things.

Anyway, you now need to start thinking about how it was that Joseph and Mary and Jesus ended up in Gebel Qussqam in Egypt. It was not by chance. You must realise by now that we all follow the complex steps of a merry dance and that coincidence is an unlikely misstep. No it was Pharouk who had helped to plan the escape into Egypt when he discovered the terrible situation the family were likely to face, In his extensive travels across The Levant he traded with all the key merchants and kings and religious leaders. He was a man who could provide them with weapons and another with jewels; he knew all the secrets and key contacts to ensure that the plans of the rich and mighty were able to develop. He knew where to get the best lapis lazuli for the lowest price and where to sell it at its highest selling point. He knew where to get saffron or garlic or nutmeg. If you wanted myrrh then he was the key man to know. His long apprentice as a dirty, ugly little urchin who was despised and ignored and overlooked had helped him get into places where more noble and noticeable people would not have access. It was not that he was overly trusted to start with; it was simply that his ugliness rendered him as invisible. He deliberately wore scruffy clothes of no colour; he always stayed in the background as a matter of intellectual choice. It had started off as a matter of simple survival and developed into a key strategy to help him develop into his role as the most important trader across the entire area of what is now called the Middle East. Not bad for a boy who was attacked and permanently damaged by a tiny little parasite.

Pharouk knew that Joseph and Mary would be able to find a solid shelter in the cave at Gebel Qussqam and had suggested this to his Magi friends to pass on, He knew it would be a good location for their exile whilst the Holy family waited for Herod to complete his rather evil lifespan.

So the perception people had of Pharouk was largely based on the fact that his face was wildly scarred and his eye socket screamed out the fact that his eye was missing. Because of this people thought the very worst of him that he was somehow unclean and must nurture evil intent. Pharouk had the audacity to look different and seemed not to ashamed to share his disfigurement with anyone who dared to look. He was brazen and surely must be uncomfortable to be with.

Yet, in the end, he was very successful. He had made the very best contacts across the whole of The Levant. All the great and the good sought him out because he could get goods of quality that no-one else seemed able to obtain. You could trust the quality of his items and the price and the date and standard of delivery. He offered a good customer service at a time when such matters were still in a developmental stage. He had integrity and any dealings he had that needed an element of secrecy remained as unspoken and immutable.

It was rumoured that he was able to perform great deeds himself with the materials that he traded. Indeed, there was no better person to obtain good quality quicksilver or brimstone from that the enigmatic "Pharouk the Souk" ad he was later called.

Confusion is like a mist that occurs when you are walking down a well known path and then suddenly find yourself in a place that you did not expect to be. In fact you realise that you may never have been there at all and yet you still have to find your way back to where you came from. However, you never actually make it back to the starting place; it is just a different location to start another journey from. Kit the man found all this to be quite scary but Little Kit the cat was not worried by this at all.

Pharouk was able to use his scarred face to his advantage, it helped to sow the seeds of confusion in those he traded with. You do not need to have the mind of a detective cat to realise that very little in this universe is anything like what it first seems.

10. Consider Protons

Proton fact: Experiments were conducted on the surface of the Moon by the Apollo team to seek to prove their proposition that over ninety-five percent of particles in the solar wind are electrons and protons, in approximately equal numbers.

There are 7,000,000,000,000,000,000,000,000,000 atoms in each and every human. Kit has not counted them himself but trust that clever humans can do simple adding up well enough even though that is quite a lot to count out. If you times that by all the millions of people in the world then you will see that there are some serious figures of human to consider. They have a lot more than the number of protons that constitute the cat population, but considerably less than all the fish swimming around. So, some you win and some you don't win. For example if you weigh all the humans on earth and all the ants on earth then you will find that there are far more ant atoms than there human atoms even if you discount the fact that ninety percent of human atoms are not really human at all. Your world turns on such mysteries. These boffins have even worked out how many oxygen carbon and hydrogen particles are broken down into protons, neutrons and electrons, It is quite a lot of particles for you to juggle every second of every hour without you even realising what you are doing, You should all be very proud of yourselves.

At the moment the most accepted views among intellectual humans is that all of the protons in the universe were formed very soon after the so called "Big Bang". Now given that Kit was very aware that this Big

Bang never actually happened he considered this to be a flawed proposition. Well, you would, wouldn't you?

So the majority of scientists and experts nowadays seem to be happily accepting that at this particular starting point of the universe there was no stuff at all anywhere, just a lot of loose energy zooming around everywhere in the form of nice little photons, which is their name for particles of light and also some larger particles called bosons. These early bosons consisted of energy and lots of them broke apart into protons and anti-protons. Most of these protons and anti-protons eventually lost energy and hooked back up into bosons again, but some of the anti-protons seem to have gotten lost somewhere, and all the mass in the Universe comes from these left-over protons. Well, when you explain it like that it all seems very simple doesn't it? It does not seem to them that there is some underlying master-plan that helps to explain why this should happen. They seem to prefer a rational that says it is all some form of chaotic randomness.

Of course all protons, everywhere in the universe, are seen as being exactly the same, and pretty much all of them are inside atoms. Different atoms have different numbers of protons; what makes an atom become a humble atom of helium, or a rich atom of gold or an atom of oxygen seemingly depends on how many protons it has, not what kind they are. This means that you will be just the result of some simple mathematics rather than a great deal else. Just a few silly old atoms different and you could easily be a cabbage,

You will probably know that all these experts are telling you that all protons are actually made of even smaller invisible particles that have been named as quarks. Each proton has three quarks: these consist of two up quarks and one down quark. Like a tiny genetic maisonette. Like birds of a feather quarks stick together by virtue of a strong nuclear force. Because a proton has two up quarks and only one down quark, it has a positive charge, like the positive end of a magnet. Two things that have positive charges push away from each other, so the protons in an atom are always pushing away from each other. They need things called neutrons to pull them all together. The neutrons help to stick the protons together as a result of that strong nuclear force Kit mentioned earlier. There certainly seem to be a lot of old forces zooming around all over the place.

Now the reason that Little Kit is banging on about protons and quarks at this point in the book is all because of the Holy Spirit. Using his highly developed skills as an astral travelling ancient spirit and amateur detective he could very clearly see the obvious connection that could be made here.

The Holy Spirit was rather a strange old thing who had been around from the start and generated energy and movement as it proceeded from host to host. Kit did not know whether to call the Holy Spirit "he" or "it"; the phenomenon was never really seen as particularly feminine but he did not wish to seem sexist and so Kit usually decided to stick with "It". Kit tried hard to be sensitive about such matters in a world of constantly changing perspectives.

Little Kit was not an arrogant sort of cat. Even though he had lived for millions of years in millions of life forms he really did not think of himself as being particularly clever. In actual fact the opposite was true, he had realised from very early on that he actually knew very little of the truth about anything at all. For example he knew invisible forces like gravity and physical attraction existed, but he would not be able to speculate too much into the how and why of such things, or anything else, Kit would just ask his questions and seek to dig deeper. What he did know what when he was being spun a whole lot of ill informed nonsense by supposedly clever men. He feels that you are more privy to lies and deceit and ignorance than people ever were before, and humans across all of "so called" history have always been subject to lots and lots. He had a belief that was called "The Great Lie" and hopes that you can follow his expression of this fundamental aspect of his personal being. Little Kit has always felt his mission has been to expose the truth wherever he can, but has found it a much more difficult task than you might think.

11. Consider Paraphernalia

Paraphernalia Fact: The word paraphernalia described miscellaneous items of equipment used for a specific activity most often those considered to be superfluous. The word is said to come from the 17th century to describe the property owned by a married woman.

After Little Douggie Hiscox and his wife Amelia had died the house that they were living in was emptied, ready to be sold onto whosoever it was that wanted to live there. All of the furniture was taken away and sold at an auction. Most of the household goods were given to a charity shop. There were just a few plastic bags of miscellaneous belongings that were given to their son. These were items the house cleaner thought might be of personal interest and were at a level that was just above too good to be considered as actual rubbish but not good enough to be of interest to anyone else.

Little Kit accepted the few plastic bags and gave them a cursory glance but was not particularly interested and so just placed them at the back of his shed intending to return to look through them a bit more thoroughly in the near future. It was actually three years later when he finally got around to the task. He recognised most of the items that he found in the bags. There was a foot long orange alabaster figure that used to adorn a family drawing room. It was made by Aarons and Son of Mare Street in Hackney and was part object d'art and partly utilitarian flower vase. It was a genuinely ugly item that the Aarons family had travelled around Britain selling in market places from Pontypridd through to Newcastle hoping to find householders who had no taste and a willingness to purchase pretentious tat. There was a small leather pouch that had Doug's Army records all brown and disintegrating with age now. Remember that all things burn in oxygen, including us.

There has to be a particular point in time when the marvellous bright red shrunken head of John the Baptist that was a hugely powerful receptacle of the Holy Spirit turned from being the greatest possible treasure known to mankind into being rather obscure and useless piece of paraphernalia that was discarded into the back of a scruffy little shed in a suburb of

Cardiff. At one point it was the focus of all desire by the richest men in the world and later became a rather despised piece of household rubbish. Little Kit is often musing on how big things become little things and how little things become big things. At one time the Holy Spirit was seen as being very important indeed, more marvellous than many of the other greatest Gods of mankind and all of the holiest beings imaginable. Now it has been consigned to history as seemingly useless, obsolete, irrelevant and unwanted. Oh well, it was all very sobering to contemplate, but that was not going to get a small monochrome cat any kippers was it?

12. Consider Psychiatry

Psychiatry Fact: It might surprise you to learn that all of psychiatry is simply guesswork by supposedly clever people. There are no scientific tests that can prove any mental health disorder any more than they can prove or disprove a possession by evil spirits. To a small black and white cat like Little Kit all of psychiatry is just complete nonsense that forms a small element of the ongoing marketing campaign that forms the "Great Lie".

You probably do not read the Bible. No-one really does anymore. However for quite a while over the past couple of centuries it was quite a popular pastime. For many families living in Europe it was the stories from the scriptures that they grew up listening to and forging their moral compass directly from the tales they were told. As with all such matters there will always be voices who question the validity of the source material. That is how an inquisitive race like humans really ought to be. Well done.

Now there are many interesting bits and bobs dotted throughout these books and there are two in particular that relate to this particular book. Both have to do with severed heads. Now cutting off someone's head is a pretty brutal sort of action and for those who undertake this practice it nearly always causes them to consider matters of morality and dislike. After all, most people do not go around chopping off the heads of people that they like, do they? Severing heads has consequences for both parties involved.

So the two cases Little Kit wants to draw your attention to are firstly the reported fates of the giant called Goliath and, later on, the demise of John the Baptist. Both have been pretty well know stories in the past but do not seem to come up in too many conversations nowadays.

Most people seem to forget that Goliath was actually beheaded. Somehow the slingshot taken by the young David has always stayed in the public memory and secondary the detail that the smaller man rushed forward and chopped the giants head off seems to be romantically forgotten. This tells us something about us all. What would psychiatrists tell us? Was David simply bloodthirsty? It really proved to be an exceptionally good career move for someone of such tender years. Kit knew that the ancient soul Pugnance was pretty busy at that time going around possessing Israelite and he really hoped that she had nothing to do with all this.

So what does the Bible actually say about the last moments of John the Harbinger? The fuller account can be found in the sixth chapter of the Gospel of lovely little Saint Mark which reports the events in the following way:

"A convenient day arrived when Herod spread an evening meal on his birthday for his high officials and the military commanders and the most prominent men of Galilee. The daughter of Herodias came in and danced, pleasing Herod and those dining with him. The king said to the girl: "Ask me for whatever you want, and I will give it to you." Yes, he swore to her: "Whatever you ask me for; I will give it to you, up to half my kingdom." So she went out and said to her mother: "What should I ask for?" She said: "The head of John the Baptizer." She immediately rushed in to the king and made her request, saying: "I want you to give me right away on a platter the head of John the Baptist." Although this deeply grieved him, the king did not want to disregard her request, because of his oaths and his guests. So the king immediately sent a bodyguard and commanded him to bring John's head. So he went off and beheaded him in the prison and brought his head on a platter. He gave it to the girl, and the girl gave it to her mother. When his disciples heard of it, they came and took his body and laid it in a tomb."

There is quite a lot of information to consider here. It does not actually name the girl, but it has long been thought to be Salome. You will appreciate that if for some reason it was not Salome then that is a terrible legacy to have been foisted upon her. Experts say it is because John was critical of her Mother for marrying her second husband. That is a bit "rich" considering all the questions arising from his particular family, but nowhere is it written that humans need to be consistent with their judgements.

If you were offered a gift to the worth of half a kingdom would you just have wanted the head of someone who might have made you grumpy? It seems pretty doubtful. Then it was seen that the body was collected and buried, but it does not say what happened to the head. What do you think the Mother of the girl did with the head? What do you think she wanted it for? Do you think it was just thrown away after the buffet with the falafels and sweetmeats? Of course it wasn't. So the ongoing fate of the head of John the Baptist is a key element in this book because, as you have already discovered, it ends up in a quite unexpected place. Also, it was not just any old head. It was a great deal more than that.

Before we go on to consider the ongoing situation of the severed head there are just a couple more points Little Kit needs to bring to your attention. You will have seen that this particular chapter is called "Consider Psychology" and he wants to spend a few moments now to allow you to reflect of how this pseudo-science has been developed. We now live a world where science and chemicals and synthetic substances dominate the world of medicine. In the greater scheme of things this has really not been the case for very long. For millennia there have been shaman and herbalists and medicine men and various crones who have all known secrets of healing. Even now you can go to the jungles of Equator or the Mountains of Tibet and find people who can teach you to travel on the astral plane. There are people who can cure cancer in Brazil by the laying on of hands and chanting sacred words. This has happened in all great civilizations and societies throughout all of time, and yet now it is seem as gibberish and rubbish. Fair enough. So you put your faith in modern chemicals found in the science laboratories of money making organisations, Kit can tell you that this makes no sense to cats who just laugh at you. So humans come up with wonderful names for the illnesses of the mind such as schizophrenia or psychosis and they explain them to each other and argue what each means and how they can best be overcome. They think they know how the mind works. Of course, they actually know very little. It is embarrassing how ignorant all these clever people are. Your human world is full are charlatans and you really need to understand that they cannot be trusted. It was not that long ago they were covering people in leeches and talking about the four humours. We are still there. You understand that Little Kit is quite passionate about this matter because he has been drawn to the surface as a result of organic mental imbalance, and he has experienced the quackery of these experts first hand.

Next you need to think about the gifts that the three wise men brought to the baby Jesus. As you will surely know, these were gold and frankincense and myrrh. So who are we thinking about these here, what strangeness links these three diverse objects to the subject of mental illness? Just think about gold. Now you humans are usually pretty sketchy when it comes to the matter of gold. You know there are lots of stories asking, what happened to the Ark of the Covenant or what happened to the wood on the cross? Little Kit thinks these are good questions that he might have asked himself in any other circumstances. Then there are issues around the true bloodline of Jesus? He was a carpenter but you never hear of anyone seeking to find a chair that he made. Even more strangely, given that humans are essentially the most possessive and greedy creatures in all existence, you never hear of anyone asking questions seeking to discover what happened to the gold that Jesus was given? Surely, you have to think that is odd, don't you? Also you really should be thinking a little bit more about myrrh. What on Earth is it? It sounds like something that you might cough up unexpectedly if you eat a sausage roll the wrong way.

Yet these are mere sidetracks to the main narrative of this story where Little Kit has to tell you a bit about a soldier called Alabast. Now he is crucial to this particular tale and is someone who probably should be mentioned in the Bible, but is probably quite glad that he isn't.

It is not particularly well know anymore, but it was common knowledge in the past that the personal guard of King Herod were made up of a regiment from a region called Thrace. It is now called Bulgaria and they formed a significant part of the armies of Gaul. The Thracians had long had soldiers who were fighting in the Roman Army and they had joined the service of Herod after he overthrew Antigonus to become the King of Judea. In actual fact they had been the bodyguard to Cleopatra and were gifted to Herod after the battle of Actium. However we do not want to get too bogged down in history at this point as we have an awful lot of that to wade through later on.

When King Herod said he wanted to have the head of John the Baptist given to him on a plate it was very clear that someone would be expected to do it. After all it was not as if Herod would dirty his hands by actually swinging the axe himself is it? By and large rich people left all that kind of ugly work to lesser mortals. Just as they still do to this day. So it was that Alabast in his role as leader of the royal guard of King Herod became the man who had to chop the head off from the torso John the Baptist.

Alabast was not a particularly cruel sort of chap, he had got into a few scrapes in his youth, but he considered himself to be a good soldier. In his view the main quality of that profession is that you do exactly what you are instructed to do by whoever it is that pays your wages. Of course he had some qualms, it is not every day that you get asked to chop off the head of a living prophet is it? Particularly at a birthday party when you are least expecting it! However he was the man for the job and so he quickly got John the Baptist into the best possible kneeling position and gave as hefty a swipe of the axe as he could muster.

It was quite a bloody business and Little Kit will not go into all of the details as it might upset some readers, and that is the last thing he would want. Some of those present said that they heard the noise of a mighty wind, others suggested the presence of doves but Alabast himself never spoke of the incident ever again. Psychiatrists nowadays might say it would have been better is he had "opened up" and "shared his feelings". However Alabast was pretty sure in his own mind that the whole ugly business should simply be forgotten and that his name should not be associated with the event at all.

13. Consider Perfume

Perfume Fact: All emotions can be smelled. Male humans, like all other mammals can smell when a female is ovulating.

Of all of the senses you have to agree that it is smell that has got the rawest deal! You hear of families who will travel miles to see a pretty view, or of people who will consider taking long journeys to hear their favourite music being played. However, it would be surprising to learn of a family who were getting excited at the prospect of spending a weekend piling into a car to go and smell something that was located somewhere else. Indeed, people do not even go out of their way to take a sniff of things that are located nearby. It really does not seem very fair at all does it?

So then you have to ask yourself, how would you explain how a cabbage smells to someone who has never actually encountered one? It is harder than you think. It is one of the strange things about ancient spirits that smell actually forms a usual part of their discussion when they unexpectedly meet up at various points in their journeys. They will tell each other where they have been and what they have been doing and exchanging gossip, as you would explain.

Then there nearly always a general point scoring exchange where one will ask the other, so what the nastiest thing that you have smelled. This is because they actually want to tell their co-traveller about something nasty that they have encountered and is the opening gambit of the conversation that allows them to do this. In Little Kit's case is was the toilets in the Hotel Amir Kabir in Teheran the late 1960s, but that is information from a different story that does not have particular bearing on the matter at hand.

So you know there are lots of very pleasant smells in the universe and an equal measure of unfavourable odours. For our purposes we are going to have to take a slightly detailed look at the role of Frankincense in our world. Firstly it is a very interesting subject in itself also it has a direct bearing on the detective work that Little Kit needed to undertake to get to the bottom of this case.

Frankincense is produced by slashing through the bark of the tree and causing bleeding. The sap comes out in tears to form the resin. It is said that the tears arriving from the last of the taps will produce the finest aroma. Quite a lot of religious imagery seems to be wrapped up in this simple process don't you think? What do you think Jesus did with the frankincense that was given to him by the Magi? Well, it turns out that he ate it. How unexpected is that?

The ability of the human race to smell has seriously deteriorated over the past thousands of years. There was a time when a person could trace another person's pathway across land simply by following am unintended scent. Hunters could easily discern where the animals they were seeking could be located. In a time before food was labelled it was useful to know if produce was still fit for consumption. Children could wander off into the forest or the deserts and still be found. There was a golden age of human smelling and it is now long gone.

Pharouk, Jesus, John the Baptist and all your favourite Old Testament prophets used to small of sand. No matter how much they washed in the River

Jordon or larked about in the Sea of Galilee of even gutted the fish they caught, it was the smell of the rocks and soil that permeated everything. That is one of the reasons why frankincense was important. Like church bells of today the sweet scent of the burning resins would act to invite believers to the holy places and temples. The alchemist would occasionally smell of sulphur, the camel traders accepted the odour f their beasts as an occupational hazard. However, at the setting of the sun each day it was the smell of sand that filled the night air all over the region and was the first odour that carried on the wind over the land when the sun forged its way into the next tomorrow,

Whilst humans have lost the ability to small their own feet the system is very different for cats! There is a good reason why our feline friends like to take a slow stroll around their elected neighbourhood and it has a great deal to do with sensory overload. A cat can detect all the information nature chooses to deliver in this way. The wind will tell them of the weather today and tomorrow and even a long range forecast. The air will explain to the cat any messages that the flowers and trees and grasses exchange across both the narrow and broader ranges as required. They can detect the messages unfolding from the soil and the rocks themselves. Of course, all cats leave messages and the gossip of the day can be located to see who has slept with who and what each other had for dinner and who has eaten all the kippers. Humans now use television and newspapers as a key form of media communication but cats prefer the old ways. In general cats have discovered that there is less "fake news" and exploitation in the trusted ways of nature.

14. Consider Performance

Performance Fact: The brain of an octopus is smaller than its eye.

So far in this book we have not really considered the skills Little Kit has developed as a detective. He was the sort of cat who liked to consider things from a range of different angles. Being able to travel in time and space was normally a great advantage but the fact that he was now using the damaged brain attacked by organic failure did cause problems. It meant that he could not remember all the facts he wanted and everything seemed to merge from one thing into another without any logical reason. Still he was a determined little feline and was not going to let these inconveniences deter him from his enquiries. He would find out how that wooden box ended up in the shed in Cardiff if it was the last thing he would ever do.

To the sensitive nose of a cat frankincense is actually quite a smelly old resin that has been traditionally used by human in the making of perfumes and incense. It is probably best known for being given to Jesus when he was born and it was also used when his body was wrapped at the point he died the first time around. In the animal kingdom it is only certain snakes that enjoy being around the small, all insects and birds have a great dislike of frankincense in any form.

There are actually not many trees left that produce the tears that bleed out to produce this resin anymore. It has rather lost its popularity. You might not be aware that ancient peoples thought the trees that produced the resin were considered as miraculous as some can grow directly out or hard rock without any need for soil. These trees can also survive the most ferocious storms and it was thought this was just one form of magic that could be transferred to humans.

Whilst there has been a record of a type of frankincense being produced on the mainland around Arabian Peninsula for well over six thousand years this is not the most powerful source. The genuine trees of pure resin can be found only on the little island of Socotra, a place of ancient and unique biodiversity off now located off the coast of Yemen. The trees are protected by snakes and so the milking and gathering of the sap is conducted only by the bravest and those of pure heart.

Of course frankincense was recognised as the most important of the consecrated incenses offered to the Tabernacle when it was located in both the first and second Temples in Jerusalem. Just as Jehovah was considered sacred as the name of God so it was that frankincense was viewed as the sacred smell of the one divine Almighty God. Those who gathered the true frankincense were considered noble and were to be venerated and honoured. This had been explained to those who inherited the Earth from the instruction of the angels. It had been proclaimed that only kings and high priests should be allowed to prepare the sacred holy resin for the holy rites of true worship. Of course, this instruction was forgotten and abandoned over time and it was inevitable that the power it evoked would significantly decline. To all ancient people it was well known that true frankincense is dangerous to harvest because of the venomous snakes that often live in its branches.

One trouble with writing a book that has emerged from a place of onset madness is sometimes there can be interruptions that infringe the logical process that is normally adopted. So Little Kit apologises for this, he does not do this to upset the reader, but he hopes that you can understand and are sympathetic to this situation.

Those who are privileged to arcane wisdom are completely comfortable with the notions of universal attraction. When you buy a cabbage at the market you think it is a random sort of event. You think that it was a question of choice that you happened to fancy a cabbage on that day and that it could have been any old vegetable that you selected. That is really very, very simple. Just as you may think that the cabbage is just laying there and could have been picked up by anyone. That makes you a random man. This is the kind of thinking that was the simple lot of Kit the man when he was only pathetically human. It was the arrival of Kit the cat in his psyche who taught him the greater profundities of the greater wisdom. It was inevitable that the paths of you and the cabbage would coincide; it was preordained in space and time. The cabbage was grown and picked and travelled hundreds of miles through various merchants to be in that market and on display at the very same time that you had travelled from your house into the market to that particular stall to select that particular item. Mankind has lost its ability to see the profound. Almost all humans are so wrapped up in evidence and logic and science that it seeks to decry the much wider fundamental mysteries that encompass us all. Angels do not sit around wondering how many humans can dance on the head of a pin. They know the answer, every human whoever was and whoever will be can join in the merry dance. There is plenty of room enough for us all.

So do you think it was a coincidence that the three wise men brought the gifts of gold and frankincense and myrrh? You know it wasn't. Do you think it a coincidence that Jesus was born in Bethlehem, which fulfilled an ancient prophecy? Of course it wasn't! We have records of the censuses of the time, there was no need for Joseph and Mary to have travelled to the town of Jessie for bureaucratic purposes, that is a mere devise that has ben written into the gospels to hide the deeper truth.

You will realise that all other creatures in all spheres get along quite nicely without having to understand a formula of pi that tells them how a cycle works. So what is E equals MC squared, it will still do that even if it has a name, if it really does that at all. Quadratic equations are all very nice and everything is wonderful in the world of numbers. However most creatures exist quite contentedly without having to know their times tables? You really do need to consider how bacteria know where to go. Bacteria do not arrive at a point out of sheer randomness, and if a simple organism like that can get the wider picture then why can't you?

Well that is just probably forcing us a bit too far ahead in where we are going. For the moment we need to consider the issue of the "Philosopher's Stone". As you know, alchemy has been something of a quandary to human thinking. It is all very romantic to consider the "Elixir of Life" and a substance that will change base metals into gold and all the usual gothic drama that plagues the honourable and noble practices. As always with human thinking it is the need for some evidence and logic that has got in the way. So how would you feel if Little Kit the cat told you one day that the true "Philosophers Stone" is quite simply holy blood? Of course there are many different types of blood and some are more powerful than others. In the particular case of the head of John the Baptist it is the resin made from the sap of the dragon's blood tree that proved to be the feature that helped him begin to solve the mystery of how the head got into the shed.

This is another of those places where you need to understand a little bit more about how the ancient souls can astral travel. It is quite a hard discipline to learn because there are always interesting aspects that you find along the way to sidetrack you. This particular journey was no different; there are a million paths to follow. For this particular journey Little Kit decided to follow a quest using melancholy as his primary guide. \he thought it proved to be quite a fun little exercise and he is hoping that you will be as entertained as he was.

So you will know that John the Baptist was the cousin of Jesus who went around dunking people in water and helping them find a direct pathway to God. Now given the scarcity of resources in that region at that time that was viewed as a pretty good power. Inevitably there were lots of people around who were pretty keen to own the power that John the Baptist had. You can imagine that can't you? As far as Kit the black and white cat could tell it is the energy of overwhelming greed that actually makes humans tick.

There was this particular chap called Philip. Like most of us history has largely passed him by, but there is still a faint trace for those who choose to follow. He was not the brother of Herod who was known as Philip the Tetrarch who reigned over a place called Ituraea and was the uncle and first husband of Salome. No this was a totally different Philip altogether. He was Philip the Alchemist and he was the one who ended up in possession of the head of John the Baptist and arranging for a wooden box to be made to house it in.

At the same time we need to think just a little bit more about what we know of the life of Jesus. We know he was born in Bethlehem and was given some very nice presets. He then went off to live in Egypt for a few years. Nothing much is known of his childhood. He turns up again as a youngster at the Temple in Jerusalem and amazes all the wise men with his knowledge. He then disappears off and nothing is heard until he was thirty. At this point we know he is a carpenter, that he can do miracles, that he has followers and that he can consider lilies. People say that he is the Son of God and later on that he was the King of the Jews. He then is killed, rises again and disappears off into the heaven to sit with God with whom he is a third. So far, so good! Yet there has been a lot of speculation about those missing middle years. Did he just stay in Nazareth and Capernaum and make chairs and door frames and all the stuff carpenters do. He certainly seemed to have an understanding of some of the great wisdoms and so there is speculation that he might have gone to India to learn from the sages there.

There is no particular record anywhere to support that view.

Kit, having the ability to astral travel, had the possibility to pop over and meet him and find out form himself what exactly was going on.

The first thing that Kit discovered was that he quite liked the weather over there. The dry sandiness suited him pretty well and he felt very content with the warmer climate. The second thing he discovered was that Jesus was and is exactly what people say he was and is. He really was everything to all men. He really was the cabbage that came to say hello and feed you. He was the most ancient of souls and the newest of souls, he was at one with all things and he was separate in his own right. He was all the labels that had ever been allocated to him and was more beside.

Kit the black and white liked to think that he knew a bit about everything because he was an ancient soul who had lived millions of lives and travelled throughout all of time and space pretty extensively. Kit had studied with the great masters and lived in rock and gas and sea and air. He had flown with the stars and shone through rainbows. Let's be quite clear, Little Kit had really been around the block. Yet he knew that when he met Jesus he was just a simple bacterium in comparison. He was a germ and Jesus was quite simply the master alchemist. Jesus was the blood and he was at the same time the "Philosopher's Stone". Little Kit was not at all religious and had never actually felt awe before, not even when he lived through the creation of the universe and saw the birth death and resurrection of all things. However, he knew quality when he saw it and he could tell the Jesus was pretty special. For a little while they would hang out together and talk about local basketball teams and swap recopies. Then Jesus said that he had work to get on with and Little Kit was following his melancholic trail. Still, they were nice days that he remembered with fondness.

Because Jesus already knew everything he was not particularly bothered in what Little Kit had to say about him finding the head of John the Baptist, even though it was his favourite cousin. Kit felt that Jesus was a little bit annoyed with Philip and what he had done, but you know Jesus, he never really complained too much. He was actually a bit of a saint when it came to that sort of thing. Little Kit came to a realisation that omnipresence and predestination is sometimes a bit of a curse.

Anyway, so there he was over in Palestine either side of the time when yet another year dot would happen and all the calendars of the West went back to nought again. He was following this line of melancholy and he had discovered that the head of John the Baptist had been given to the mother of the exotic dancer and then to a chap called Philip the Tetrarch who was both her uncle and her first husband. He knew that the Head of John the Baptist was a pretty special sort of trophy and handed it over to the safe keeping of the chief scientist of his court who was Philip the Alchemist. Now he was instructed by his King, who was the one who paid his wages and paid for his equipment, to seek to harness the power of the Holy Spirit located within.

Philip the Tetrarch ruled the land called Batanaea from its capital Caeserea Phillippi, which happened to be virtually the most northern place that was visited by Jesus. It is one of those very specific locations identified in the Bible where it says:-

"When Jesus came into the coasts of Caesarea Philippi, he asked his disciples, saying, who do men say that I the Son of man am? They said, some say that thou art John the Baptist: some, Elias; and others, Jeremias, or one of the prophets. "

It is one of those coincidences that Little Kit did not believe in that Jesus should be talking about his cousin on his travels in the very place where John's head would end up. This was before it was shrunken and placed in a gopher wood box and started to turn a very bright shade of red.

Vibrations are of fundamental importance to us all. Now Kit the cat fully understands that quite a lot of the notions he presents are quite difficult concepts for humans to understand. He realises that at this particular point you might be quite vexed. All these things had taken him an eon to come to terms with, so in the comparatively short allowance of time you have currently experienced then there is no possible chance that you can grasp the complexities of the Great Cycle of Being. Of course, if you have been an ancient soul at some point then things would be clearer, but the chances are that you would not remember, that is the way of these things.

So the first very difficult idea is the reality that there is no such thing as time, well not in the way that you understand it. Let's face it; you have absolutely no idea where time comes from, what happens to it and where it goes. However, this particular point of the universe is quite different to the one that was presented to an hour ago, or yesterday, or five years ago. So how does that work? Well it is simply a matter of vibrations. All of our lives and deaths and conscious awareness and movement and senses and space itself is formed around the variation of vibrations. So we are surrounded by contradictions. At one level matter exists whilst at exactly the same point matter does not exist. Thought, feeling, emotion, relationships, song, wind, all aspects of all of creation emanate from a single point and are also everywhere across the universe at one and the same point. All positivity and negative are completely intertwined. Imagine a simple line drawing of a wavelength on a piece of paper. If you have a wavelength that goes up and down, then you can easily see there is an equal wavelength that corresponds down and up in harmony. You also have all the white parts of the paper that surrounds the wavelength that it is moving though that needs to be there to hold the wavelength in place on the page. You also have the act of drawing the image and the desk the notepad is on and the production of the tree that the wood came from to make the paper and the iron that was used to hold the desk together and the room the desk is in and the house the room is in and all the air around that sustains life in the house and outside too. Then there is the Earth below that the house is sitting on and the planet the at this surface layer sits on and its relationship to all the other planets around it and the space it is moving through and all the magnetic force fields and clack holes of the universe and the forces of gravity and time and its journey through space and its relationship to the place it came from and where it is going. So from a simple squiggle on a page you can see that it can relate to a whole bunch of other things. When you get to grips with the concept you will learn to understand that it relates to everything and that would include the fact the scribbled line does not exist at all except in your imagination. Like everything else, it's easy enough to understand when you get the hang of it.

Of course Little Kit the cat had actually met John the Baptist on a couple of occasions. He did not really like him as he found his a bit to vehement in his arguments. The first time came before he started his ministry and he was known just as John is those days. He had been sitting with the young Nazarene fisherman that Kit was living in at the time and was saying how cruel the people in the village were about his Mother. They saw her as a "batty old women" who thought she had been in conversation with some visiting angels. There was very little in the way of political correctness around at this particular juncture and sometime people could be very dismissive and cutting. Little Kit tried to be sympathetic, he knew things were about to get a bit worse for the youth. He tried to explain to him how the simple power of moving water can assist in the fundamental principles of sharing glory. It was quite a simple idea but John was not really paying attention, he obviously was a bit more interested in making a name for himself. They went on to talk about basketball as both lads were keen on the local rivalries that existed in the towns and villages around.

The next couple of times their paths crossed came a bit later. John was already quite a popular figure in the area. He used to rant away at a point of time when there was no television or many other leisure activities. So there he was standing waist deep in the rather dirty water and encouraging all the people who had come to see him to come to him so that he could dunk their heads under the water to enable them to feel the zeal of the Almighty. It has to be said that the water did not look particularly clean but you know what Palestinians are like, and they bravely gave it a go and everyone said it was jolly good and a nice day out. Of course, the Roman's around were a lot less pleased, they did not want Palestinians taking a day off work to go and get washed somewhere. There were no trade unions over there and, like at every point since colonial invasions became popular, there were quota's that needed to be completed.

15. Consider Pathways

Pathways Fact: The entire universe is made up of pathways and this includes you. As just one example a biological pathway is a series of actions among molecules in a cell that can lead to a change in the cell. It can trigger the assembly of new molecules, such as a fat or protein, turn genes on and off, or even spur a cell to move.

Now this is a very difficult chapter and you will need to concentrate a lot to get from this point to the end of it. Little Kit has tried his best to help introduce a few key ideas about alchemy and some of the people who have helped to shape the story of the box with the shrunken head. They are not people who actually knew each other, but all of them were featured in the "Path of Melancholia" that was being followed.

Little Kit would politely suggest that all of the characters included in this story are either victims or perpetrators of some level of persecution. In most case they will be both at different times and in differing situations. To a cat observing from the outside this seems to be one of the sad realities of human existence. You are all like this.

.   A little while ago in this story we left Samuel Pallache being returned to Amsterdam having been imprisoned by the British who had accused him of illegal piracy, among other things. This had come at a time when Plymouth had quite a lot going on what with disappearing giants, new drainage systems, Pilgrim Fathers, Frances Drake, Pocahontas a nice new synagogues and everything else.

There has been an interesting book written about Samuel called "A Man of Three Worlds "which chronicles his move from being a consultant and diplomat within the court of the Sultan of Morocco to becoming a commercial consultant in Holland and then a spy in Spain. It was in the earlier part of his life in Morocco when he first gained procession of the shrunken head of John the Baptist. It would be nice to say that he received it as part of a payment for honourable work conducted on behalf of the Sultanate, but that was not the case. He obtained it by more unsavoury means. Unlike the other Muslims and Jews in the court he had been born in Spain and suspected the old gopher wood box might be of great value in Catholic Spain. At that point he did not realise what the contents of the box might be. To him it was just an ancient container that was clearly considered important to the alchemists who employed him. Samuel did not them know that this was one of the most cherished objects in the entire world and that ownership of it would place him in the most severe danger. Just as those who had held the head before had always been in fear of their lives, so it was that Pallache innately knew he had to keep his treasure to himself until the political timing was perfect. The knowledge was projected out by the power of osmosis. However, these were particularly treacherous times to navigate. It was dangerous enough just being a Jew, let alone one who was in possession of one of the most significant artefacts ever to come out of Palestine.

The journey of a normal sized head of usual dark skinned Middle Eastern colouring to becoming a much smaller, small great fruit sized head that was bright red in colour was of itself an interesting trail Little Kit had followed though his astral travelling.

As you know, it stated not Far East of Jerusalem when one of the daughters of Queen Herodias danced in front of her uncle, King Herod the Great. As a reward he gave the head to the girl who may or may not have been called Salome. She in turn then gifted the head to her Mother who was the one that had made the unusual request. How this is when there is a bit of a problem with names as the great historian of the time known as Jehosephat noted in vexation there were lots and lots of Kings called Heard and Philip and some called Herod Philip and lots of intermarrying between their various wives and offspring. In Kit's experience this was the sort of behaviour that never leads to anything helpful.

Goodness knows how or why it happened, although Kit had some suspicions, but Queen Herodias almost immediately gave the severed head to her brother in law, King Phillip the Tetrarch. The head quickly made its way up to Caeserea Philippi. It became very clear to Little Kit in his following of the "Pathway of Melancholia" that the head ended up in the stewardship of Philip the Alchemist who lived in a place which is nowadays in Northern Lebanon. He was a wise old chap who was largely retired from the court of the King and was largely left to his own devices conducting all of the usual experiments that alchemists seem compelled to do.

Some three hundred years away from this Little Kit had spent time in a town called Panopolis in Egypt with a very interesting chap who was called Zosimos. He was Gnostic mystic who wrote about the work of the earlier alchemists who he followed. In his book "The Quest for Elements" he seems to have offered one of the first definitions of alchemy as the study of "the composition of waters, movement, growth, embodying and disembodying, drawing the spirits from bodies and bonding the spirits within bodies."

Aside from his writings Zosimos was mainly known for his studies in metallurgy and his interoperation of the visions he had. He understood the principle that every action has an opposing reaction and for each positive element there is a negative counterpoint. These are very ancient sciences and it was believed at the time that they came from a previous civilization. According to the Apocryphon of John and the Book of Enoch it was the fallen angels who first taught the art of metallurgy to the women they married. Metallic transmutation—the transformations of lead and copper into silver and gold—was seen as a process with a spiritual dimension. It always needed to mirror an inner process of purification and redemption. It is a reflection of the "Divine water" the name of the sulphurous water used by alchemists.

It is quite a hard concept to grasp and Zosimos once explained it to Little Kit in this way: the alchemical vessel is the baptismal font and the tincturing vapours of mercury and sulphur were purifying waters of baptism which helped to perfect and redeem any initiate who wished to follow Gnostic practises. The mixing bowl, known as the "krater", is a symbol of the divine mind in which the Gnostic initiate was "baptized" and purified in the course of a visionary ascent through the heavens and into the transcendent realms.

Like most other alchemists Zosimos firmly believed that the timing of an experiment would strongly influence the outcome and so he used to bang on endlessly to Little Kit about what he called "timely tinctures" which meant doing certain things at a particular time in a synchronistic relationship to the zodiac and the position of the planets.

In those days visions were taken very seriously indeed. It is not like today when everyone seems to think that they do not matter. Zosimos used to have all these dreams about alchemy which were considered to be both heavily symbolic and weird even by those who followed his teachings. Zosimos was often granted visions by a small black and white cat who suggested wondrous things. He was instructed that sometimes water is not water and that there are occasions when blood might not really be blood at all!

In his most discussed vision Zosimos got himself involved in a big nasty old fight with a chap called Ion whose claim to fame was that he claimed to be the founder of the Sabian religion. So in the vision this Ion fellow fights Zosimos with a sword and impales him. Ion then disembowels the unfortunate alchemist and pulls the skin off of his head. Ion then burns all the different pieces of his body on an altar so they are transmuted from body to spirit. Then Ion cries tears of blood and melts horribly into something unpleasant. In his writing Zosimos describes this new being as "the opposite of himself into a mutilated anthroparion". After this dream Zosimos wakes up and ponders everything that happened and just goes back to sleep. Meanwhile the vision is continuing without him and back at the altar someone is being boiled alive and in his excruciating pain cries out "This is the entrance, and the exit, and the transmutation. Those who seek to obtain moral perfection enter here and become spirits by escaping from the body". Throughout all of this Zosimos feels himself to be drifting in and out of sleep. He then dreams of a "place of punishments" where all that enter immediately burst into flames and submit themselves to an "unendurable torment." Well we have all had dreams like that haven't we?

He then describes a snake eating itself. This was the Worm Ouroboros and is still a well known symbol of the unity of everything. Another thing that Zosimos used to be very keen on discussing was mirrors, He saw these as a way to explain the contemplation of the divine self and the experience of the Gnostic sense of the Holy Spirit rather than to see a mere reflection of the material self, It started quite a trend among alchemists which carries on to this very day.

These were times when all humans very firmly believed in other spirits and their assorted tribal explanations of the creation of life. It is pretty difficult to just be surrounded by nature and not want to have an understanding of what it is you have been dragged into. So it is no surprise that Zosimos, like everyone else at that time, firmly believed in demons and angels. He suggested the view that these were quite limited in their outlook and only had knowledge of the specific part of the cosmos where they lived and it was only the creator of everything that had knowledge of the whole of everything. He used to try and complete his works at a very specific time of the day or night in keeping with comprehensive understanding of both hermetic and Gnostic concepts of divine contemplation to help ensure that his assorted undertakings achieved the best results.

Those who become masters of the art of astral travelling will know there are a trillion different paths that can be followed. This could be simply air itself or a particular emotion or perhaps a suitable person or even an individual spirit. The list of possibilities is simply endless as are all the atoms in the universe that can be trailed. The fact that Little Kit had chosen to follow melancholy as a linking guide was purely based on his vast experience of such deliberations. Well there was a whole lot of melancholy to work through at the time of all the many different Herods and Philips.

Anyway, the severed head of John the Baptist was kept in a nice box that was specially made from gopher wood. Little Kit had been following a trail that went around the countries that surrounded the Mediterranean Sea and it was not firmly located for nearly a thousand years as it passed through the hands of the leaders of various secret societies that were primarily interested in alchemy and the "Elixir of Life".

It was finally traced to be in the secret treasure house managed by a Muslim intellectual called Maslama al-Majriti. His full name was Abu 'l-Qāsim Maslama ib s'lama al-Majritin Aḥmad al-Faraḍī al-Ḥāsib al-Majrīṭī al-Qurṭubī al-Andalusī but he was known as Maslama al-Majriti for short. He was quite a big name in the circles of famous alchemists who was born in Madrid in the year 951.

Al-Majriti was another of these "renaissance men" who have seemed to have popped up in this story. Yet this was at a time before the renaissance happened; clearly a man ahead of his time. To be a bit technical he was most noted for editing and changing parts of quite a wonderful collection called "The Encyclopaedia of the Brethren of Sincerity" Which was one of the first know attempts by scholars to consider the damage caused to us all by "The Great Lie". Some people suggested that the bits he changed did not need altering at all; others thought that the entire book would have been improved if all of it had been changed. Well, we all know that humans can be quite cutting with their petty criticisms don't we?

In his mind Little Kit always referred to this most famous of alchemists as the "Marshmallow Man", perhaps it was just that he reminded him of something squidgy: he really could not remember why he had used this nickname. Al-Majriti also predicted a futuristic process of scientific interchange and the advent of networks for scientific communication. He promoted advances techniques of triangulation and surveying and so he was considered to be a very wise man indeed. He built a school of Astronomy and Mathematics and marked the beginning of organized scientific research in the region. He introduced and improved the astronomical tables and aided historians by working out tables to convert Persian calendars. It all seemed very useful at the time, but not to a small cat whose interests tended to rest elsewhere.

Nowadays people are not particularly bothered about things like secret powers and curses. This was not always the case and it would be a very brave man indeed who would feel that they were able to open the ancient box of Philip and confront whatever doom it might reveal. It was for these fears that the artefact had remained closed for over nine hundred years. It was when he was just twenty-three years old that Al-Majriti felt confident enough to go to the Treasurer and in the darkness of a sacred space finally managed to reveal the hidden relic that lay within the box.

Of course he was utterly shocked. He had not really known what this most mighty treasure would reveal and the very last thing he had expected is that it would be would be the shrunken head of the cousin of the Christ and the distributer of the gifts of the Holy Spirit to man. He had been expecting that it might be a hand or a foot, and was certainly not thinking that the crazed eyes of a decapitated prophet would be staring out at him from a bright red shrunken head. As brave as he was it sent shivers down his spine. Well it would, wouldn't it?

You will remember that the shrunken head of John the Baptist was bright red. This was because when the box to contain it was made the alchemists of Philip's court had added the resin of the dragon-blood tree of Socotra and it had been absorbed by the induced osmosis of the preservation processes. Of course Al-Majriti was not aware of this procedure and he later sought to recreate the process. As a result he became one of the earliest alchemists to record the usage and experimentation of mercuric oxide.

Al-Majriti various works included many alchemical formulae and instructions for purification of precious metals, and was also the first to note the principle of the conversion of mass, which he did in the course of his path breaking experiments on mercuric oxide which generally made things of another colour turn bright red. He took natural quivering mercury, free from impurity, and placed it in a glass vessel shaped like an egg. Then placed this inside another vessel like a cooking pot, and set the whole apparatus over an extremely gentle fire. The outer pot was then heated forty days and night. When opened the mercury which had weighed a quarter of a pound had been completely converted into red powder, soft to touch, the weight remaining as it was originally.

Little Kit had originally thought this was the reason why the shrunken head had turned bright red but later discovered the real reason had been the decision by Philip the Alchemist to add the resin of the dragon-blood tree into the box many years earlier.

As you would expect the box with the shrunken head of John the Baptist stayed in the treasury and at his death was passed on to the stewardship of his astronomer daughter Fatima of Madrid,

What happened next was a little bit more difficult for Little Kit to follow. He had heard rumours of the trophy being held in various locations all across the Mediterranean area, certainly it had passed through Thessalonica and Turin before moving onto Marrakech, Rabat and Fez. As far as Kit had been able to understand from his investigations that had been no actual sightings or evidence of the relic and its presence was simply the stuff of myth. That was until a certain very clever Pope came onto the scene.

16. Consider Pope Callixtus II

Pope Callixtus II *fact: He was forth the son of William I who was the Count of Burgundy and one of the wealthiest rules in Europe.*

It was not as if Pope Callixtus II had actually touched the box but it was his actions that made things far more difficult for anyone who owned a genuine relic to say that they had it in their procession. It was his work that increased all the secrecy that surrounded all holy objects in his desire to confront simony. It is not a particularly pertinent matter in current times but in the twelfth century it was a pretty big issue.

Simony is described as the act of selling church offices and roles. It is named after a bloke called Simon Magnus, or "Big Simon" to his mates who ho is mentioned in "The Acts of the Apostles" as being the opportunist who offered two of Jesus' very best disciples a large payment in exchange for their empowering him to impart the power of the Holy Spirit to anyone on whom he could get his hands on. Now this was the very reason why Philip the Tetrarch had wanted to acquire the head of John the Baptist. He had thought that if he could obtain the power that was located in the head of John the Baptist he could control the Holy Spirit to undertake his will and also obtain a great deal of gold from selling this power to those wealthy rulers who could afford it.

By the time Callixtus II got to become the Pope there was a lot of peculiar financial exchanges taking place as the church became increasingly corrupt over the centuries and the term simony extended to embrace other forms of trafficking for money in spiritual things. Simony was one of the important issues during the so called "Investiture Controversy" which he was able to settle through the amusingly named "Concordat of Worms" in 1122.

Because he was part of the noble aristocracy of Europe he was in indirect family member of many of the other people that Little Kit had encountered on the pathway of melancholia. This includes all of the Mendoza family line, Juan Ponce de Leon, Amelia Aarons and all the others including the man whose soul was possessed by a small cat. It sounds unlikely, but you need to remember that we are all connected at some point. You just need to dig around to find the links. His real name was Guy de Bourgogne. Who would have thought that the world had a Pope that was originally called Guy?

In 1088 under unusual circumstances Guy managed to become the Archbishop of Vienne. This was a time when such positions were deemed as important. Before that he was not yet even a cardinal but having ties with noble families was very useful in those days and he was duly elected as a Pope at Cluny on 2nd February 1119. Nine cardinals took part in the election as most of the other cardinals were in

Rome. He was crowned at Vienne on 9 February 1119, as Callixtus II.

In 1120 Callixtus II issued the papal bull which was called "Sicut Judaeis" that set out the official position of the papacy in respect of the treatment of Jews. It was all tied in with the First Crusade, during which over five thousand Jews were slaughtered in Europe. The papal bull was intended to protect Jews and echoed the position of the first of Popes called Gregory that Jews were entitled to "enjoy their lawful liberty." This seemed all very decent of them. The bull forbade Christians, on pain of excommunication, from forcing Jews to convert, from harming them, from taking their property, from disturbing the celebration of their festivals, and from interfering with their cemeteries. As this took place in a period where such diversity was not always universally popular it can be seen as all being very commendable indeed.

The millions of tiny signals and vibrations converged to make this became just the right time to hold the Concordat of Worms. It was all very political and really quite interesting but had nothing much to do with the box containing the bright red shrunken head of John the Baptist

In order to secure the confirmation of this Concordat of Worms Callixtus II convened the First Lateran Council in March 1123. It solemnly agreed the recommendations of the Concordat and passed several disciplinary decrees, such as those against simony and the long standing issue of the presence of concubines among the clergy. Decrees were also passed against violators of the "Truce of God", along with church-robbers and also all forgers of ecclesiastical documents.

So you can see that there really were some jolly bad people hanging around in those days.

It goes without saying that the "indulgences" that had been already granted to the crusaders were renewed and the jurisdiction of the bishops over the clergy, both secular and regular, was more clearly defined. So he was generally considered as being quite a good Pope in a period when not all pontiffs were quite so readily appreciated.

Although it was a very serious offense under church law the practice of "Simony" had became simply rife in the Catholic Church throughout the ninth and tenth centuries. Kit's old drinking buddy John Ayliff later wrote:-

"Simony is defined to be a deliberate act or a premeditated will and desire of selling such things as are spiritual, or of anything annexed unto spirituals"

Most people nowadays are not really interested in such matters but that has not always been the case. Thanks to the zeal and efforts of Pope Callixtus II the wicked practice was subsequently massively diminished. Of course, the head of John the Baptist was just the sort of thing that could be exploited for financial gain and so the crackdown on the business of selling miracles would have been a concern to anyone who wanted to take advantage of a thousand year old head.

Callixtus died in December 1124. He devoted his last few years to re-establishing papal control over the so called "Roman Campaign" and establishing the primacy of his See of Vienne over the less pleasant See of Arles which had been one of those ancient inter-church conflict that required resolution. Little Kit had mixed feelings when the news of his demise had come along. In general he had not been a great fan of Popes, he had always found they seemed a tad pompous and "holier than though" and we all know that Kit was essentially an egalitarian at heart. All in all if Little Kit had been asked to sum up this chap in one word he would have said "pink" and he knew already that pink was his least favourite colour.

You do not have to be a genius to work out that being in possession of a holy relic such as the head of John the Baptist which had the power of the Holy Spirit firmly placed within it was putting the owner at potentially very great risk indeed. Even if the owner was entirely pure of heart and had no evil intentions it was a time when the ownership of relics was considered by many as quite a risky undertaking? These were not enlightened times compared to those that we are all living through nowadays!

17, Consider Partition

Partition fact: Gondwana became the largest piece of the crust on the face of Earth before it became an even larger supercontinent called Pangaea. Gondwana and Pangaea gradually broke up to give us the basis of the still moving continents we have today.

Little Kit had lived many thousands of lives in many different forms and he could remember as far back as when alchemy had started. It was not like what it is in these days. The humans of this world had been created with an inbuilt programme to be obsessed by gold and that influenced everything, as you will know only too well. No in the very ancient civilizations the alchemists had lived by a different code and had asked very different questions. It would not be uncommon for one to spend a lifetime considering where compassion had come from; another might be completely devoted to discovering the secrets behind homing instincts. They were very interesting times and the planet was a happier place for it. Of course Kit had been an alchemist on quite a few occasions, usually as women as it happens, and he had quite enjoyed the focussed life that path followed.

Of all the many, many thousands of lives that Little Kit had lived and existences he had experienced there are a few that stand out as his favourites. There would be a range of different reasons for this, some were people he genuinely liked, some he found particularly amusing or interesting, a number were fascinating and others tragic but provided a touch of pathos. Many were victims of injustice some were intriguing, many were complex and a few were relatively simple. From across this entire range the one that hold the most relevance to this particular adventure was a merchant called Pharouk. Now he was quite a dark skinned fellow who was born on the island of Socotra which was then, and still is, located off the coast of Yemen. This was not always the case. At one of those times when the continents were all jumbled up in different places. The small patch of land that became Socotra was a tiny part of the ancient supercontinent of Gondwana. Then all of the land of the planet got itself into a state of agitation and started to dance merrily off into the distance. Socotra remained the same whilst everywhere else changed and this is why it is now considered as a place of particular scientific interest.

Indeed a huge amount of the flora and flora of the island can only be found living on the once happy little island that minds its own business in the Gulf of Arabia.

There is a large cave in the caverns of Haq which is known to the locals as the home of those who fell. Not too far away from there is a large flat area of stone on the floor that is covered with ancient runes and primeval sketches. It is like a fallen story board. To those who know how to read such things it is a map of future events that tells the tale of treasure and of secrets.

The greatest treasure that was given by the Magi was not gold, nor myrrh or frankincense. It was not the knowledge of moving stars. It was not the bowing of the knee by men of greatness; the greatest treasure was simply the keeping of a secret. We all know that had any of the three wise men decided to pop in to see horrid King Herod they hw would discovered who had born as the new king and where he could be found and he would have been killed. Had this happened all the other firstborn of the region would have been saved and out history would now be very different. We are told that the three Magi were told in a dream not to go and visit Herod. It does not tell us who had this dream. They were wise men, it was not a dream, and it was part of the prophecy that had been told to them by Pharouk. He had learned the story as a child having been instructed by his Grandmother to read the runes and patterns from the stone floor pictures on the island of Socotra. The greatest gift that was given to the baby Jesus was not even mentioned, and certainly not venerated as it should be. Until now poor old Pharouk has been totally forgotten in the annals of history,

To be fair, in his reporting of these matters St Matthew did not bother to give the name of the three Magi. Indeed it is open to translation if the three Kings were even kings at all. They are also deemed as wise men, following stars being quite a clever thing to do apparently. Even the timing of the visit is open to speculation as it could have been any time from the moment of Mary pushing to up to two years later. All the nice Christmas cards seem to have a clear idea of the timing of events and tradition is somehow fooling us all. So we must rely on unnamed scholars who, quite frankly, are a wee bit "dodgy" as they are influenced by their own personal history in just the same way that we all are.

The word "Magi" is a term used to denote that a person is a follower the Prophet Zoroaster. It is thought that the earliest known use of the word Magi is in the trilingual inscription attributed to Darius the Great which is known as the "Behistun Inscription". Actually "Magi" is an even older word used to describe a person who is a practitioner of magic. This would also include related subjects like alchemy, astrology and astronomy along with all other forms of esoteric knowledge. Later on the travelling Greek gentleman-soldier who was called Xenophon wrote that magicians were considered to be the authorities for all religious matters and they were the ones given responsibility for the education of the emperor-to-be.

Originally the Magi were seen as the interpreters of omens and dreams, but this altered over time. When the Greeks started writing seriously *"mageia"* was used not for what actual Magi did, but for something related to the word 'magic' in the modern sense; that is using supernatural means to achieve an effect in the natural world, or the appearance of achieving these effects through trickery or sleight of hand. Little Kit was used to seeing a degradation from the profound as humans became increasingly frustrated with their inability to understand the true secrets of the world they lived in. You do not have to dig much deeper to see this is still a practice that continues widely still. One of the consequences of this was that the Greeks' image of Zoroaster would metamorphose him into a magician too. One of Kits favourite Greeks was an old boy who eventually ended up with the name "Pliny the Elder" who was bumbling around in the first century when all that good stuff was happening and he wrote that. In his view, "Zoroaster" was actually the inventor of magic. So making wild claims is nothing new. You should all know that were it not for a strange change in weather conditions all of Western Europe would have been followers of Zoroastrianism, but that is the stuff of a different story.

Little Kit was a frequent visitor to Greece in those days and can confirm that the Greeks became absolutely obsessed with the many strange notions that prevailed around different types of magic. Pliny said that magic was a "monstrous craft" that had brought about peculiar lusts and an endless craving to discover its secrets. He accused many of the more prominent Greek philosophers, including both clever little Plato and noisy old Pythagoras, of simply travelling abroad with the sole purpose of studying magic and then returning to teach it in order to seem "special". Pliny thought they should have used their obvious intellect to consider more serious matters and invent better political systems for the rest of humanity to follow. According to Pliny all the great academics of the day were all obsessed with learning more about necromancy.

So the wise men who came to see Jesus after his birth were certainly Zoroastrians and probably magicians. Do you think they might have performed tricks in the stable for the newborn baby? Well, probably not! The real question is how much do you think Jesus would have known about Zoroastrianism? It this is the kind of thing that interests you then Little Kit would suggest that you might want to dig just a little but deeper. It certainly was the sort of thing that interested him.

18. Consider Positioning

Positioning fact: The ancient Chinese understood that energy is a constant force in the universe, and surrounds us in everything that we interact with. Feng shui was developed as a means to harness that energy in the best possible way to ensure positive outcomes.

Little Kit had a problem. He had a favourite thinking place which was located over the back lane and under a scruffy small bush. Here he would like to sit in peace and solitude in order to embark on his astral travels. Now h=it had always been a place that the other cats in the neighbourhood had respected as a site of holy sanctity. None of the other cats around particularly liked Little Kit, but they were quite proud of his chosen way of life and commitment to whatever strange thing that it was he was doing. That had been the case ever since he had been rescued and brought into the area. Yet things were changing. One day he went to follow a lead on his current investigation and he was horrified to find that someone had used his favourite resting place as a toilet. This then happened a few days running and he realised that it was the big black cat from the house at the end of the lane that had deliberately expanded his usual routine in order to defile his chosen spot of holiness.

Of course his was the handiwork of Pugnance. She was now in the life form of the black cat that lived further up the back alleyway. It had been a few years now since she had followed Little Kit into the suburb in Cardiff. It was something of a habit. To Kit it seemed like she had nothing better to other than trail the various paths that he took just in order to try and annoy him. It had started hundreds and thousands of years ago and continued all across the universe. It was a pattern. It seems that whenever he had got himself settled in a new form and built up a nice quiet routine for himself to enable him to pursue the various detective tasks that Pugnance would turn up! It appeared that he would just settle in and set himself and then, a few months or maybe even years later up she would pop with her sneering and cruel jesting with the single task of spreading mischief.

Little Kit had built up coping strategies; the main one was to seek to ignore her as that was the response she seemed to dislike the most. When he reflected on it he had surprised himself to realise that on those occasions when she was not nearby je actually quite missed her. Well, he would certainly never be telling her that!

Whereas Kit would tend to describe himself as a detective he knew that Pugnance would usually call herself a "reader of souls" How pretentious was that! Begrudgingly he would say that she did have a genuine talent to getting to the heart of the people she had set he sights on possessing. It was as if she had a natural empathy that attracted her to those who were weak willed and defenceless. However Kit felt that she had disrupted all of his handiwork quite enough and had decided not to dwell too much on her presence. He still had a story to try and complete.

So this now becomes another of those points where Little Kit thinks that he needs to add some more bones to the picture you may have of Samuel Pallache. In the late fifteenth century, many of the Jews expelled from Spain made their way down to Morocco where a number of long established Jewish settlements existed. In some areas they were consigned to areas that nowadays might be called "ghettos". However it can be seen that among many of the larger towns they had established more dynamic communities. One such place was Fez which was the city that had become the home of the Sultan of Morocco. A number of Jewish families became prominent in commerce and public life there. Among the Jews of Fez of Hispanic origin was Samuel Pallache. He served the Moroccan Sultan as a commercial and diplomatic agent in Holland until his death in 1616 and he plays a key part in this story.

After the left Fez and moved to The Netherlands he became increasingly unsettled and despite the inquisition and exile realised that he really wanted to return with his family to Spain. To us this makes no sense, but the lure of the place you consider to be your "home" is one of those invisible magnets that can defy simple logic. So Samuel decided that he should try to convert to Catholicism to help assist this process. In those days changing faith was a pretty big deal, but to those in the Jewish community of Western Europe it was often a matter of survival as it has been in other places at other time too.

History tells us that Samuel abused his trusted position to work as an intermediary which allowed him the opportunity to spy on Moroccan affairs for the Spanish court. He became an informer for the Moroccan court against the Dutch and the Spanish, he then informed on both the Moroccans and the Dutch to the Spanish court and informed on the Spanish and Moroccans to the Dutch court, This was a golden age for informants.

As we already know he later became a privateer against Spanish ships and was tried in London for that reason. Nowadays employers praise the ability of their workforce to exercise "transferable skills". Samuel Pallache was pretty cute at all this adapting malarkey. His religious identity proved to be as mutable as his political allegiances. When in Fez and he was devoutly Jewish; when in Amsterdam he was Jewish or Protestant as the situation demanded, when in Spain he was a loyal *"converse"* which is the term they used for a baptized Jew. It might seem to any historian that he was simply duplicitous but the reality was that his entire family could only survive by changing allegiances in the turbulent geopolitics of the time that he lived in. Like Pharouk he was a man who was not a member of the aristocracy and yet he had important dealings with many of the most important leaders of the age.

Samuel Pallache had personal dealings with the Ottoman Sultan the Marinid Sultan, King Philip III of Spain, King Louis XIII of France, James I King of England and Prince Maurice of Nassau as well as the leaders of the Netherlands, none of whom are particularly well known for their love of dealings with those of the Jewish persuasion. No one seems to know that he was in possession of a small old gopher box. Well, Samuel was very good at keeping secrets.

19. Consider Parenthood

Parenthood fact: In the animal kingdom Orang-utan mothers act as single parents for eight years and will only have another baby when their young one has reached that age and can cope by themselves.

For ten years after the birth of Pharouk all was good for the family. Shebatha was contented with her lot. She liked being a venerated grandmother on the wondrous island of Socotra. Who wouldn't? It was an honoured place to be valued by the others in the community. She cared for her cabbages and goats and the days were good. She was proud of her daughter Megshaom who was starting to bring up her growing family with wisdom and integrity. She was proud of all of her children. The sun shone and God was indeed kind and all was blessed. All the clouds that came along were quickly blown away.

The trees that they tended and harvested grew quietly each year and flourished. The grazing goats played in their usual happy goatish way. There was always fish available, the sol was healthy. The various traders who ventured over from the mainland were always friendly and life was as good as life can possibly be.

Then, when Pharouk had his tenth birthday everything changed. She could not possibly know that is was an invisible wondering waterborne worm that would devastate the lives of the whole family. Who could have known? Within a few short months her lovely daughter Megshaom the Soother of Souls became renamed as Megshaom the Banshee. Soon after she was Megshaom the Cursed and that was the title that stayed with her until the day she eventually was found hanged from the dragon blood tree by the cave of the holy.

Of course, by this time Pharouk had long since left the island. He had shuffled across many lands and visited the courts of the mighty. His mother and grandmother knew nothing of the sights he had seen through the squint of his one good eye. They knew nothing of the vast amounts of money had had passed though his hands and the secrets he had been told. He was simply lost to them.

Nothing is known about the Father of Pharouk. It was almost certain to be one of the men of the clan but Megshaom never revealed which particular person it was. In those days any child born was just added to the clan and the issue of paternity was not quite as important as it seems to be with humans now. In those days there was a collective responsibility for the welfare of all the children, no matter who the actual birth parents were. The entire adult membership of the clan had a responsibility for training, chastising and playing with the children so that they could enter adulthood in order to help the entire grouping survive in times of hardship and thrive in times of plenty.

The clan lived in a happy position where a man was judged by the human qualities he brought to the community. Wealth was not really known. Everything needed to be carried from one site to another at short notice and so there was no need for property to be an issue. There was no need for fashion, the cloths needed to be practical and longevity was more important than mere prettiness. The clan needed to be fully mindful of their environment and to respect the gifts that nature provided on the island. There were merchants who came to the island who liked to collect the resins and the honey and in return gave small brightly painted pottery trinkets that the children of the clan could play with. There was no crime on the island to speak of, no real acts of jealousy as each day was greeted with joy and the routines of life were followed in the same traditions that had always been the case. The strange markings on the floor were a mystery to most of the tribe, but it was a holy and sacred area that they all venerated and treasured. The caves were venerated. The sea was holy. The trees were precious and the soil was revered. The air was filled with joy. It really was a land of bliss.

Little Kit was always astounded by the way that humans across the globe had managed to make their own lives so much more complicated and unpleasant, not just for themselves but for every other living creature too. Cats were not exactly known for their morals, but they would never go quite so far as to destroy the entire habitat of those who share the Earth with them. Even Pugnance would probably not do something like that.

The morality of cats had actually formed the basis for the ethical codes adopted by many secret societies in past civilisations. The mystery of the Sphinx is not much of mystery if you decide to look at it through that particular lens. You will have seen how the ancient Egyptians used to honour their cats and even mummify them in the hope that they would help guide the humans on their deathly voyage across the sea of the sky. As it happens the "Keepers of Aaon's Promise" were of quite a different mindset altogether. They were altogether far too wrapped up in the questions around transformation and veered far more towards minerals for their answers than to consider what has occurring all around them in nature. The bigger picture is full of smaller pictures and these smaller pictures are jam packed with even smaller pictures still and so this goes ever onwards until there is nothing to be seen at all. This is a universal truth of everything including the very notion of truth itself.

Little Kit had never really taken much to the minor deities in the times that their paths had crossed. They all seemed a bit too self obsessed and narcissistic and it came as no surprise to Little Kit that those who decided to become their followers should follow a path where they sought power and wealth and influence in the physical world rather than seeking the deeper power that was available to them in the wider reality of

119

creation. Humans just seem to grab at shiny things; they simply cannot seem to help themselves!

20. Consider Presumption

Presumption fact: You simply assumed this chapter was going to consider the issue of presumption didn't you?

When anyone begins the study of their family tree they are advised that there is a paper trail that can be followed and that these are facts. They are also advised to speak to older relatives so that the oral traditions of the family can be discovered and perhaps the facts will be verified and more flesh is available to add to the bones you are gathering. This is all good advice, unless you happen to speak to Aunty Tilly. She was one of the sisters of Amelia Aarons and was the one who told her enquiring nephew that the family were descended from the Mendoza family line. So, he spent many years looking at books and making connections. At one level it was very clear that Daniel Mendoza and Pope Callixtus the Second and the unnamed Conquistador and Peter Sellers were all linked into his family tree. Yet what is she was wrong or had said it as a joke or a deliberate falsehood. Then there are the lies to consider. All families have hidden secrets. Just because am ancient record says someone is a person's Father does not mean that he necessarily is. Infidelity is not a modern invention and then there were also more sensitive cases to be taken into play. Do you really think that everyone in Nazareth believed Mary's story about the parenthood of her eldest son? It certainly is quite an unusual claim and it came at a time when virgin births were quite unknown and unexpected.

So what do we actually know about the parents of Mary the mother of Jesus? Well, there is an assumption that her mother was called Anne and her father was called Joachim. Oddly enough, given that the bible is very keen on genealogical matters, he is not mentioned at all whereas the Quran dedicates an entire chapter to his family. He was considered as a pious and wealthy sort of chap who originally came from Galilee. He went to Jerusalem where, despite him being thought of as a good egg, the fussy High Priest of the Temple refused to accept his sacrificial offering as, due his childless state, it was considered that he had displeased God. So Joachim popped off into the desert to pray and say sorry and all that sort of thing for forty days which was the appropriate response to these matters in those days. Then he came back home and Anne got pregnant with the baby who was going to become the Virgin Mary. As a result of all this Joachim is now named as the patron saint of fathers, grandparents, married couples, cabinet makers and linen traders. Meanwhile his wife, Saint Anne is now the patron saint of unmarried women, housewives, women in labour or who want to be pregnant, grandmothers, teachers, horseback riders and miners. She shares the responsibility for being the specified saint for all cabinet makers with her husband. Of course Anne actually wanted a son rather than a baby daughter but had to make do with the Virgin Mary as God had a bigger plan in mind that she knew nothing about. Now some of this comes from the Gospel of Saint James, which some people don't like and other bits are legends and oral traditions. All of which means that there are versions of Aunty Tilly that stretch way back in time! Anyway, this is one of those points where Little Kit can get himself lost down a million paths and stray from the simple tale he is telling.

Generally speaking cats are not too bothered about this family tree malarkey. Along with every other creature in the universe except for humans they innately understand that we are all connected to each other. They understand that they are as linked to the mice they toy with and the birds they chase as they are to the big cats of Africa and the little cats of everywhere else. They know they are as connected to the trees and the grass and the fish of the sea as they are to the light in the sky and the twinkling starts. To them it is blindingly obvious. Cats would be quite saddened by the blindness of humans if only they had the same capacity for compassion that some holy people seem to have.

To most scholars the journeys of Jesus took him to the countries and towns surrounding Jerusalem. It was generally assumed that he had lived in Nazareth until he was thirty before setting off on his ministry. It was also said that he had lived in other places including Samaria, Jordan, Perea, and Capernaum. You will also be aware that there are a number of other views suggesting that he had actually travelled as far away as India in order to gain some of his insights. There are a few who think that he travelled back to Egypt where he had lived in exile after his birth. Of course there are all kinds of visions that people have had about various appearances he has made after his ascension into heaven and Little Kit was not likely to be the one who would offer scorn to suggestions of astral travel is he?

For most of those who are interested in his journeys reported in the Bible it seems the farthest north he travelled was to Mount Herman, just north of Philippi Caesarea. It was here he was said to have met Elias and Moses and did that whole transfiguration thing. Not too far away he was said to have cured a young boy of lunacy and it was also around here that he chose Simon-Peter to be his rock. It was quite a distance north-east of Machaerus which was the town just on the other side of the Dead Sea to Jerusalem where John the Baptist actually had his head chopped off. So according to tradition all of Jesus ministry took place Northwards of Jerusalem.

In many circumstance and traditions that Little Kit had observed the notion of heading northward was nearly always associated with problems. It was one of those strange sorts of phenomenon that he might have looked at in a bit more detail if any of his future lives caused him to return as a thinker. In his experience journeys to the south were generally less interesting, travels to the west were more likely to be uncontroversial and it was adventures to the East that were the most thrilling of all. Of course, he knew this made no real logical sense but it was a tried and tested observation that he had found to be a fact in his own personal development.

21. Consider People

People fact: In the cartoon series "The Simpsons" the only two characters who have a full set of fingers and toes have been God and Jesus.

Even now Socotra really is a very wonderful place. It is actually made up of four small islands and currently has a total population of about sixty thousand people. Over the years it has had many names given to it, including the Island where God's children smile. It has been the subject of many passing colonialists ever since such invasions begun and has been owned by the Romans, French and all the expected raiding culprits of the age. Due to its location it currently a well known stopping off point for the opportune marauding Somali pirates who do not cut quite the same romantic swagger as their previous counterparts in other areas. The capital is a really scruffy little town that smells of raw sewerage and consists mainly of ugly concrete shacks. Like most places on Earth, humans have tried tier best to destroy the magnificence of their chosen habitat. Of course, it is also in a region of great political and religious unrest and it is not even considered a safe place to visit.

Just over two thousand years ago when Pharouk was growing up there Socotra was still pristine and idyllic. The people could manage very well for food due to the abundance of fish, the herding of the small goats and the readily available supply of honey. The children of the island nearly all just became fishermen and were semi nomadic. They had discovered that there was a great interest in the resins that could be made from the sap of the trees that were unique to the island. So most of the population had some involvement in helping to

124

bleed the various trees and help to make the resins that the traders from the mainland were so keen to purchase. It all helped to make the island a very lovely place to be.

Whilst the traders brought in new ideas and wonderful stories it was very rare that anyone of the locals would ever actually leave Socotra. Why would they. It was one of those places where all the people were truly happy with their lot, and was the way that utopians like to believe that the world should be, Indeed, if you looked the same as other people on the island then it could arguably be considered as the best life that the world had to offer. The weather was always warm and balmy and on the rare occasion when the storms blew too heavily there were lots of caves to share for awhile to safely wait for normality to be reinstated.

Even if you were born a bit different then the community was kind and compassionate and everyone was seen as having equal value and could be accepted and contented. However, at the age of ten as his eye was being eaten and half his face was obliterated by the huge growing sore that ate into his face from his forehead to his chin poor young Pharouk did not feel contented. He was in constant pain and there was no relief. He could not sleep, he could not eat. He started to hate being in the company of others. He would be silently angry with everyone and everything. He would spend hours by himself tending to the special trees, gathering the sap from the frankincense trees and the dragon blood trees, he would prepare all the resins for the myrrh and balms and he felt as wretched as any ten year old boy had ever felt.

Other children on the island generally grew up strong and lively with their huge beaming beautiful smiles and adventitious sense of fun. This all rather passed Pharouk by. He was unnaturally small and stunted. He could not smile; it hurt, so he developed a permanent scowl and quite a dark nature to go with it. He knew that he could never really fit in on the island. He understood very quickly that he could never get to marry any of the girls of Socotra. No caring parent would ever allow their precious child to live with someone like him. It was a difficult adolescence, but one thing became certain in his mind. He was going to leave Socotra. Of course he loved him family. In his mind there could not be any two more wonderful people in the world than his Mother and his Grandmother, they were always so kind and understanding no matter how often he railed against them. He knew that they loved him.

They loved him even when the other islanders turned against them and had spoken behind their backs and started to treat them as outcasts. This was because it was believed that they had brought a curse to the island. Pharouk knew nothing about the power of microbes. In his damaged and childish view he knew it was his fault. He felt each unkind whisper and veiled insult as if it were a physical blow to his heart. They never said that they were ashamed of him, but he was ashamed of himself. So he would wonder off collecting his saps, making his resins and wondering, if he did not kill himself, just what the world was going to hold for him.

No-one could have guessed that his body would be wrapped in holy shrouds and that he would be

126

entombed in Egypt and that whilst he was being transported to the Gods in his own personal boat of a million years a modern army would come along and build their perimeter wall over the carefully selected resting place for his earthly remains. No, even the powerful prophecy of his birth and the many visions he experienced in his sacred travels failed to inform him that would happen.

22. Consider Philosophy

Philosophy fact: Pythagoras forbade his followers from eating beans.

It is Little Kit's experience that it is rare that a journey will end up where you expect it to and very often a journey might never have an ending at all. For all of her prowess as a prophet and a seer Shebatha never imagined for a second that she would end her days living in an isolated cave in the south of the island with her daughter Megshaom with both of them being estranged from their clan. As a little boy running innocently around the sacred hills of Socotra Pharouk could not have thought he would end up wrapped in the finest of funeral cottons in a tomb over in Egypt. He had no idea that Egypt even existed. Similarly Samuel Pallache could not have imagined when a young scholar in Fez that he would travel to the Caribbean and end up in Amsterdam. Just as Juan Ponce de Leon could not have guessed that he would finish his days buried in Cuba when he had been a young lad playing in the stables at his home in Valladolid.

It must have been an even bigger surprise for Fatima of Madrid to discover that she had obtained that particular name given that she had spent her entire life in Cordoba and had never even been to Madrid. The world really does spin in very strange ways.

Fatima got her nick-name as a result of her Father being known as the "Man from Madrid". There was a great deal to be grateful for being the clever daughter of one of the wisest men in the world. She was able to discuss important issues of the day and her views were valued. In fact she very quickly gained a strong academic reputation when she worked alongside her Father in publishing a number of important astronomical and mathematical investigations.

What is less well known about her is that she became the first woman to become the Great Priest of the "Keepers of Aaon's Promise". When the earliest incarnation of the sect had been established in Southern Egypt many centuries earlier most of the memberships were female participants from the noble classes. Over the years it had become increasingly male dominated and by the tenth century it was rare to see a woman at any of the ceremonies at all. Anyway, Fatima rose through the ranks from being an acolyte upwards entirely on her own merit and had the full support of those who held influence in the organisation.

As with all such groups its popularity waxed and waned with the prevailing political situations if found itself in. The stunning loss of its entire library a number of years earlier had been a very difficult pill to swallow. It is always terrible when those who seek to promote enlightenment have to face the brutal ignorance of those who constrain their worldview. There were just so n=many ancient manuscripts and papyrus texts and clay tablets and even metal books and scrolls that had simply been burned in ignorance. They were utterly irreplaceable and the wisdom taken from the word of men is an act of evil burning. It was not the first time this had happened and would not be the last, but to the scientific community in particular and the human race as a whole it was a bitter pill to swallow. However, within the treasury of the sect a number of artefacts had survived and remained as the treasure of the secret group. This included the gopher box that contained the bright red shrunken head of John the Baptist.

As the Great Priest it became the responsibility of Fatima and her counsellors to ensure the safekeeping of all the holy relics and objects of power as with all of the secrets of arcane knowledge the group possessed. It was because of her insistence that these items be preserved in safety she oversaw the removal of the treasures from their secret stronghold in Cordoba over to the palace of the Sultan of Fez. It was agreed that the relics would be much safer there than anywhere in Spain.

Fatima herself never married nor bore any children. She was an intellectual who loved her work with mathematical equations and the study of the zodiac and her experiments with base elements. Like all members of the "Keepers of Aaon's Promise" she was desperate to find the "Elixir of Life". She had no interest at all in romance or relationships or maternity; she was completely driven by the need to find the cure for all illness, just as her Father had been and all the other Great Priests in whose footsteps she followed.

Nowadays she is mostly remembered for her academic work. In particular she was praised for her advanced calculations of the true positions of the Sun, the Moon and the planets. She was able to provide more precise readings to help establish mathematical tables of sine and tangents. Fatima's fine mind further developed spherical astronomy helping to establish increasingly accurate astrological tables. Her work on parallaxes calculations and eclipses of the Moon placed her at the forefront of all the scientists of the age. Yet nowadays very little is remembered of her at all. Why do you think that might be?

Little Kit had tried to establish if she had ever actually opened to box and seen the head of the prophet. He could not find any evidence that she ever had. It is one of those things that people could ask over future generations. What if Fatima had come to an understanding of the power of the Holy Spirit that she had at her fingertips and yet so tantalisingly overlooked? Certainly the re-conquest of Spain would not have been completed and the travels to the New World might have been a very different proposition. On such small points all of history turns.

There are those who say there are universes where all possibilities are acted out. It is a fanciful notion. Imagine a world where it was not the sperm that made you that won the race to your Mothers egg but it was the sperm next to you, or the next one, or one of the other thousands and thousands rushing around in darkness. There are a lot of possibilities just there alone.

So what do you think Fatima looked like? Well the answer is that you will never know. There is no portrait of Fatima anywhere in the world. So there we have probably the cleverest person in the world in the largest city in Europe at a time of artistic and cultural enlightenment and yet not a single pictorial reminder of her exists. Little Kit remembers that she had a strangely squashed sort of face, but his memory is quite poor and it might well be that he was confusing her with someone else. There is no collage that takes her name and there is not even a plaque anywhere in Cordoba with her name on. It is as if her memory has been wiped clean from the history books. Surely, you have to ask yourself why this would be.

Throughout the time Fatima resided in Cordoba it had become one of those hubs where the great and the good of the time occasionally seem to congregate. It had an interesting history as the Visigoths took it from the Romans before it became an emirate and than a Caliphate. Indeed, Córdoba had a population of half a million people as it grew to be one of the most advanced cities in the world and a great cultural, political and economic centre. However, as seems inevitable with all such civilizations, a collapse was inevitable. In an attempt to appease the demands of the Moorish clergy the vizier al-Mansur insisted that all philosophical books be burned as they were seen as an affront to the Prophet. Then along came civil unrest. It was a very opportune decision by Fatima and he councillors to move the precious items away from the city. Eventually Cordoba was recaptured by Christian forces during the great re-conquest in 1236. However, the worm was already a long way into the apple by then.

Now if you had just three words to describe the human race what three words would you use? The philosopher Thomas Hobbes famously said that man is "nasty, brutish and short". Well, that is not quite the full story. What he actually wrote was that man outside of law and society would be "solitary, poor, nasty, brutish and short. Yet somehow since his book "Leviathan" was published in 1651 it seems that mankind has somehow misplaced the "solitary and poor" bits as they are no longer parts that seem worth remembering. To a cat like Little Kit there were very many more words that he would add, but given that any reader of this tale is almost certainly going to be human and that he always strives to be as polite a cat as possible he will resist that particular temptation on this occasion.

Of course Thomas Hobbes was a "renaissance man". Unlike many he firmly believed that all humans are basically selfish, driven by fear of death and the hope of personal gain. He suggested whether you realise it or not all of you seek power over others. So, with that in mind, just say that you had in your procession an artefact that would give you access to unlimited power what do you think that you might do? Well, this is potentially quite a frightening prospect. Little Kit was very glad the box had maintained wisdom enough to keep itself secret.

23. Consider Patches

Patches fact: Pirates did not wear patches due to them having bad eyes but because wearing them helped them see better in the dark.

Of course cabbages choose to live in patches, but we are not thinking about them at the moment.

So what do you know about the beginnings of alchemy. It is quite an interesting subject. In the earliest days, in the civilizations long before the sad one that you belong to, those who were gifted with the power of deep thought would consider issues such as the nature of bravery. One of the reasons Kit likes living as a cat is that he knew from the outset that he would be brave. It is in their nature. Similarly he knew that any life he lived or shared with any human would be a life of simple cowardice. That is the way the universe has turned. On the other side of the coin humans are far more likely to assist other humans in trouble than cats would be prepared to help any other cat that might be in distress? It seems that such things can sometimes balance themselves out. Things come in cycles and things come in patches. It has always been thus.

Sometime after the man who was possessed by Kit the cat was diagnosed with vascular dementia he discovered that he was losing his sight as well as his mind. At first it was not so bad. Things became blurred and it did not affect his day to day life as badly as you might imagine. However, that was just the start of the decline. It was not long before he discovered that if he went out in sunshine then he could hardly see any distance at all. Most of the time it was not particularly sunny in Cardiff, but when it was he tended to stay indoors. He could not see across a road, or make out if a bus was coming. Then it got worse again. It started to impact on him when indoors. He could not really see what was happening on television and could not read a book or any written information any longer. As his mind deteriorated the whole process just caused him to retreat further and further into his mind which was starting to deteriorate just as rapidly.

Of course he was not alone as there are currently estimated to be two hundred and ninety million visually impaired people in the world. That is not to say that they are all entirely sightless as the term blind relates to a spectrum of vision loss. Those who are affected by the condition may possess varying degrees of sight loss and therefore will have vastly different needs and abilities related to their personal experience of the condition. However, Little Kit the cat might have already confirmed your realisation that this is true of every single component of the process of being. None of us actually share any experience in an identical way no matter how similar it might deem. Every single heartbeat you complete is entirely unique in every way to yourself. There is no-one on Earth who had ever filled your universe in the same way that you have. Even if you are being possessed by a cat the cat will feel very differently about what is happening than you do. Remember, you are only ten percent human, all of the other ninety percent of whatever it is you are feel differently about their reality than you do even though you share your body with whatever it happens to be.

Going back to the issue of blindness you will know that there are some people who have been completely blind since birth while others may have dealt with slowly declining vision for decades. Of course blindness is a pretty big deal in the stories of the Bible. There are people who had their eyes removed and others who had their vision returned thanks to miracles. Like all such matters they can be taken as both literal events or as analogies that are spiritual lessons for guidance. You must take them in the way that best suits you. There is hope and there is loss. There is light and there can be darkness and there is light in darkness and darkness in light. We are substance and we are shadow.

Blindness is often preventable and it is estimated that eighty percent all visual impairment can be avoided or cured. Early detection is the key to combating vision loss. Sadly for Pharouk people in Socotra did not really understand too much about the tine parasite that ate one of his eyes and caused him to scratch away all the area around his infection causing the wounds which scarred his face for the remainder of his life.

It would be nice to think that with all the collective ancient wisdom of medical herbs and treatments something could have been done. Soothing ointments were applied by his Grandmother and myrrh was anointed by his mother, but to no avail. The wound had turned septic and harm was permanent. He would only ever be able to see fully from one eye and his face was a daily reminder that he was visibly different from every other young boy on the island. As he grew older and left the island on his journey as an adult the scar remained, the sight was forever lost and the fear and suspicion it generated proved to the wider universe the immense power a tiny little microbe can evoke.

As he grew in power within the ranks of the "Keepers of Aaon's Promise" who he had joined when still a teen he would often wonder how many of the others had supported his progress out of pity. He liked to think it was all because of his dedication and ability that he was eventually ordained as the Great Priest of the sacred cult, but we all like to think things like that don't we?

24. Consider Probability

Probability fact: You are statistically more likely to die on your birthday than on any other day of the year.

So what are the chances of Little Kit writing a chapter about probability? You know the old saying that there is "no such thing as a coincidence!" Little Kit had been around long enough to know that everything was part of a cycle, including you. Even as a schoolchild you would have happily learned about the four stages of a butterfly, you remember, egg, caterpillar, pupa/chrysalis, adult. Of course that is only a part of the story, where did the egg come from? Where did the adult go. Most transference across the universe is unknown and unseen. You are taught a rainbow had just seven colours just because you cannot actually see infra-red or ultra violet with your naked eye, but they are still there, along with all the other aspects of reflected light. Most of the time you cannot even see the colours you are surrounded by at all. We all know all living creatures have an aura around them, but this is not usually seen by most people. This is true of all things that involve heat. If you ever have the chance to study the ideas of Nikola Tesla then it is something Little Kit would strongly advise. In his eyes it is vibrations that underpin everything. Even the straightest line in the world is not actually straight. There is movement and there is countermovement in the place where the thing has been. There is ying and yang. There is matter and anti-matter. There is you and there is the anti you. It is the most glaringly obvious secret in the universe. Also in all the anti universes that exist across all of space and time. Countless trillions and trillions of and trillions of separations of micro seconds of smaller seconds throughout all of the cycle of time. It is all a bit too big for humans to properly grasp. Like an ant trying to make sense of an ocean he cannot see and knows nothing about.

Anyway, we were thinking about the subject of coincidence and for the purposes of this story we are thinking about the role of the laws of probability. Little Kit had no real time for these so called scientific laws; he felt that they were made simply to be broken. Of course he was not a great believer in the notion of coincidence. In fact he suspected that if there was such a concept then far more examples of its existence would be presented. In your daily lives you should be facing all manner of unexplained circumstances and most people live lives of unremitting and self determining routine. Then he also considered that everything that had ever happened or would happen or could ever be was all an entire coincidence in itself. So, what were the chances of a human inventing a law of probability?

Then there was the issue of prophecy. Little Kit supposed that if enough people made enough educated guesses then there is inevitability that some of them will eventually turn to fruition. It was not that he was overly sceptical or blinding rational, it was not simply an instinct or innate belief, it was a considered philosophy based upon the fact he had lived millions of lives and had been allocated more time and space to think about these subjects than most others.

Of course these matters often require a need to dig a little deeper. What is it that makes one person more liable to take a risk than another similar person faced with the same circumstances? If you had been Herod would you have agreed to the beheading of John the Baptist? If you had been Samuel Pallache would you have become a pirate? We have some inner expectation that people will behave and think in largely the same way that we behave and think. Now that is a preposterous notion. Why on Earth would any of us think anything quite as ridiculous as that? We have all been brought up learning different lessons in an endless variety of circumstances with a functioning brain that process information and emotions in different ways. It would be something of a coincidence if any of us actually felt the same way about anything at all. The universe is full of endless possibilities that might exist or may never even be a possibility at all. The chances are that you will never have possession of a gopher wood box containing the bright red shrunken head of John the Baptist but there is always the possibility that you might.

25 Consider Panaceas

Panaceas fact: Most significant ancient cultures will have tales of a ""Fountain of Youth"" that can restore the health of anyone who drinks of its waters. Eternal youth is a gift frequently sought in myth and related stories of the "Philosopher's Stone", universal panaceas and the ""Elixir of Life" "exist throughout the ancient world.

What do you think the "Elixir of Life" consists of? Would it really surprise you to learn that the alchemists of old used varying experiments to try and develop the formula and three of the key components in the process were gold and frankincense and myrrh? Of course they had to be added under the right phases of the moon and the correct incantations chanted and there was a need for metals and minerals to help ensure that the essential water was transformed into the living power of healing and immortality.

For a moment let us consider the properties of sulphur, as this was often a key component used by alchemists in their search for the greatest of their goals. It is an important factor because it has long been established, even across previous civilisations, that sulphur is an essential element for all life. Almost all of the most successful alchemists would have needed to include the use of sulphides in one form or another in their working practices.

Sulphur is believed to be the tenth most common element by mass in the universe and the fifth most common on Earth. The amazing properties of sulphur were very well known in older times, being mentioned for its uses throughout all ancient cavitations.

Pharouk the Soul was a significant trader in sulphur, but there were a number of noted others. At a very basic level you will know that sulphur mainly as a chemical element, It is usually bright yellow and it is essentially a smelly sort of substance altogether.

In the Bible sulphur is called brimstone, which means "burning stone". A number of references link it to the once popular theories of eternal damnation that wait for the unbelieving and unrepentant. Indeed the place they called "Hell" was said to "smell of sulphur". So you can see why many people did not like having sulphur around at all and why alchemists managed to get themselves such a bad reputation. You certainly would not like living next door to one.

According to an old treasure called the "Ebers Papyrus" sulphur ointment was used in old Egypt to treat granular eyelids. Pharouk used to try and find all kinds of tinctures and remedies to help him overcome his damaged eye, but in general they just made things worse.

Across the ancient world shaman and alchemists were fascinated by sulphur's flammability and its reactivity with certain metals. They wrote extensively about the use of sulphur in alchemical operations with mercury,

In modern days we can see how important sulphur has been in commercial developments across the globe. Its uses range from creating high quality phosphate fertilizers through to the simple act of bleaching paper. It assists from vulcanising raw rubber through to helping to preserve dried fruit. Sulphur is a key component of gunpowder but Kit does not want to take you on a meander through the pathways that train of thought would take him.

Ancient alchemists would have clearly noticed that all eggs are high in sulphur levels that help to nourish feather formation in chicks. So it is a small step for them to develop this and wonder if some variation of activity of sulphur might then be a vital component to the "Fountain of Youth". Well it is clearly true that it does improve the efficiency of other essential plant nutrients: particularly nitrogen and phosphorous. As a key component of all living cells. Including all of those that have joined together to help make up you, it might have a strong case for consideration to be considered as a base for the long sought after "Elixir of Life".

For Little Kit the entire notion of a panacea is quite alluring. His detective mind is quite sure that nothing is what it seems to be and that there is power in nothing and that the opposite can be equally true. If you tell someone something enough times then they may eventually come to believe it no matter how ridiculous the notion might be. Indeed, Little Kit is pretty convinced this is how many of the key powers that underpin the way the world is currently operated have materialised. It might be the process of great wisdom and understanding or perhaps something else entirely?

Angels might be able to hear nice music but they will never know the joy of finding a nice juicy kipper left out on a saucer. We all respond to issues in very different ways and it is just one of those differences that make us exactly whatever it is that we really are.

26, Consider Pink

Pink fact: Sunrise and sunsets are sometimes pink due to Rayleigh scattering. This occurs when sunlight travels through the atmosphere and some of the colours are simply scattered out of the beam by air when colliding with molecules and airborne particles. Another example of little things making a very big difference

Pink is a nice enough sort of colour but Little Kit is not really a fan. It has never really done very much harm to anyone by itself, although when mixed with other things is sometimes can get involved in things that might not be universally approved. Anyway, like all other colours it is just a vibration. Simple as dimple! So why do you not see a nice shade of pink added to the list of colours that makes up a rainbow? Somehow red, orange, yellow, blue, green, indigo and violet seem to have got themselves headline billing and poor old pink is rather left out in the cold. Perhaps some people might think that it really isn't there. However a rainbow is a spectrum of light and so all colours are included in their somewhere. Remember there are no straight edges anywhere in the universe, not even in the human imagination, so a rainbow does not just jump directly from green to indigo, there are lots and lots of blurry little colours in between as the vibrations seek to move across the range. It is a very important lesson that small cats want to teach to humans; just because you cannot actually see something does not mean it is not there! The human eye will only see a certain amount of anything. Say you are looking across a room and there is a chair in the far corner. So you really think that there is nothing between you and the chair?

There are millions and millions of things between you and any other object. It might be invisible air, or invisible heat or invisible radio waves, or invisible emotions or invisible moments. There will be air-borne virus, bacteria, memories, hope, despair, dust and anti-matter. The air itself is full of the vibrations of all of life and all of death. It reverberates from all of the movements there has ever been or will be. All music and art and poetry and dance are here. All artistic endeavours and every destructive impulse fill the gap. Every breath ever breathed in and breathed out can be found in the very fabric of everything. We are all completely connected at every single level whether we want to be or not. It is full to the brim with dreams and thoughts. It is chock-a-block full of smells and the memory of sounds. It is bursting with gasses and radiation. It is a place where all kindnesses and all cruelties can be traced. In this space you will discover completeness and solitude. All of humanity is rested here along with the actions of the fallen and of those yet to come. In the space across your living room which you perceive as emptiness you can discover the word of God, the light of the holy spirit, the darkness of evil, the colours of the cosmos the macro and the micro. All you need to see them s to know how to look.

Humans do not know how to see what is in front of their faces. Humans are stupid Ask anyone who is owned by a cat and they will tell you that cats will often see things that are not there. This might be because they think that cats are stupid, which you may appreciate, is not quite the way the rest of the universe judges these things. Quite simply you cannot have an empty box. If you take a box and tip it us and suck all the air out of it and seal it up you will still have a box full of something, there is no escaping it. This is the simple truth of a humble cabbage, when you believe that you have seen everything a small change of

143

perspective spectacularly reveals that there is always plenty more to see.

When the head of John the Baptist was separated from the body of John the Baptist there was a lot of blood that quickly drained out. So the actual colour of the face of John became strangely pale from the dark olive colour that it had always been previously. It stayed pale even when it was shrunken in order to fit into the special gopher wood box that had been especially made to hold it. The long black hair of the prophet stayed black. It was the alchemist called Philip who decided that the relic could be improved by adding the resin of the dragon-blood tree into the box. It was not something that he had done before, but it was an educated guess that it would enhance the longevity, power and appearance of the new relic that he was preparing. The head started to turn pink fairly quickly. It was quite a long time before it could realistically be properly called red.

Pink is the favourite colour of most microbes, and of most fish. According to the Gnostic texts pink is said to be the favourite colour of God, but Kit had always suspected that it was really the colour of gold that God preferred.

27. Consider Portals

Portals fact: The "Gate of the Gods" at Hayu Marca in Peru consists of two archways that are cut into stone. The larger one is 22 feet square and inside it is a smaller one that is seven foot square. The ancient Inca people believed them to be portals. Such items appear all across the ancient world.

As you can imagine Little Kit has a very deep interest in portals, There are lots of people all over the world who seem to be unconvinced by the conventional explanations for the mysterious ancient sites and seek to find alternative reasons for what their real purpose might have been. So there are notions that there are portals which allow various bodies to move from one place to another. There are things called stargates and wormholes in time and all sorts of challenging ideas and suggestions. Kit thinks that humans should be more enquiring and hopes one day that they will start to ask the right questions and find some truth in the answers they obtain.

In the meantime he knows this could be one of those red herrings that will take him away from the focus of this tale which is how the box with the head of John the Baptist ended up in his shed in Cardiff. Yet there is just one more thing he feels would help in his following of the "Path of Melancholia" that he is using as his guide. He could have used quartz to make this point but he has elected to choose mercury, as this is more frequently associated with the work of the alchemists. Pharouk traded in many different items but it was mercury that was probably the main source of his income and was the key to his trading empire.

So what is it that is quite so important about mercury? Most alchemists at that time thought of mercury as the "First Matter" from which all metals were formed. They believed that different metals could be produced by varying the quality and quantity of sulphur that is contained within the mercury. The purest of these was gold, and mercury was needed in attempts at the transmutation of impure metals into gold.

Mercury is used commercially in a whole host of useful devices. Red vermillion pigment is obtained by grinding natural cinnabar or synthetic mercuric sulphide.

You will be fully aware that mercury has been often found in Egyptian tombs from before the year 1500 BC. Experts say that the value of the substance was known for over three thousand years but we all know it goes back eons before that. Little Kit was there when his wonderfully named Egyptian friend Khumarawayh ibn Ahmed ibn Tulun was happily rocked to sleep every night on air filled cushions which floated on had a bath filled with mercury. In retrospect this did not do him an awful lot of good but it was probably worth a try wasn't it?

Beyond this mercury has been found in the pyramids of Mexico and in various sacred sites of Peru. As just one example a small lake of mercury was built in a chamber sixty feet below the wonderful "Temple of the Feathered Serpent" which is the third largest pyramid of the incredible Teotihuacan complex in Mexico. It is no coincidence that a selection of jade statues was found there too. Alchemists were quite likely to use the same materials at all points around the globe even though they had no obvious methods of intercommunication. Well, that is to those who fail to appreciate the reality of astral travel.

On the other side of the world the first emperor of China known to his followers as Qin Shi Huang Di was buried in a tomb that contained rivers of flowing mercury on a model of the land he ruled, representative of the rivers of China. He died in great pain after drinking a liquid mercury and powdered jade mixture created by alchemists that caused liver failure mercury poisoning and brain death which was quite at odds to the intended aim of providing him with eternal life. You have been instructed to know that the best laid plans do not always run quite as smoothly as even the most meticulous and cunning of us might want.

Further forward in time the Greeks used mercury sulphide in their ointments whilst the ancient Egyptians and Romans used it in cosmetics... Way across the globe in sunny Mesoamerica at an old city called Lamanai the brightly decorated Mayan's had built a pool of mercury which they used for divination. Smaller quantities of liquid mercury have been recovered from tombs and other ritual locations in ancient sites on every continent.

The use of mercury in ritual practices is closely associated with the working demands of alchemists. Even Fatima of Madrid was known to have had a decorative pool filled with mercury in her study area in Cordoba. This was so elaborate it boasted its own fountain of her beloved quicksilver. One day she truly believed that this would surely help her to discover the elusive "Fountain of Youth"?

Quicksilver is relatively rare yet occurs in deposits throughout the whole world. The mines of Spain, Italy and those in the Balkans are just a few examples of places that have provided mercury to alchemists for well over three thousand years, Of course the alchemists saw it as a means of obtaining everlasting life and means of healing all of the ills of the world. It was a substance that would provide great power and could be used for the good of all. Nowadays it is used for somewhat baser purposes.

Unfortunately one of the many side effects of mercury is that it can have seriously adverse influences on your mental health. The vapours from the metal were well known to cause the affliction that called the "Mad Hatter" to be so named in the felt making industry. It was also not uncommon for alchemists to appear exceedingly strange and peculiar. This would have been exacerbated when they were "speaking in tongues" and chanting spells and drinking strange concoctions. Yes, it has always been quite a challenge to be an alchemist even in the most enlightened of times. Little Kit was able to reflect that portals do indeed come in many forms.

28. Consider Parents of John the Baptist

Parents of John the Baptist fact: Zechariah the father of John the Baptist is noted in The Koran as a prophet. Some Muslims believe him to have been a martyr following his being sawed in half.

Now in order to understand this book you might need to know a little bit more about John the Baptist. Of course, before he began baptising he was just a plain old straightforward John, and there were lots of those hanging around all over the place. There is a school of thought that says he was definitely an older cousin of Jesus and there are those who say he was actually no relation to him at all. However, we should all know by now that all things are connected and so we can safely say that they were connected in some way, just as they both are to us today. The whole discussion is simply a matter of degree. Anyway there are some things about him that people do largely agree upon. There is a consensus that he was the son of a chap called Zechariah Ben Jehoyada whose trade was being a prophet, John's mother was called Elizabeth, and she was not a saint at the time he was born but was deemed as very special indeed and gained her deserved title a bit later on. It is believed that John never married and had no children no siblings and so the bloodline of the Ben Jehoyada's ran out at exactly the point his head was chopped off. It is pretty well documented that his parents were quite old at the time he was conceived and so were well gone at the point of his demise. Looking back on events it seem perhaps killing someone to end an entire bloodline is somehow worse than killing someone who has prodigy to carry on the family name? Morality is occasionally burdened by such vexations.

Anyway, John was one of those people who were very closely in touch with the Holy Spirit and so he started a ministry in the River Jordon where he would happily baptise anyone who thought they needed it. Luckily for him there were lots of people in the area who really wanted to be baptised and so everything was going along quite swimmingly, so to speak.

It is universally agreed that John baptised Jesus, an act which casing talking doves to come along. This caused later controversy as some people thought it would be quite unnecessary to wash clear the sins of the son of God who apparently had no sin, but that is the sort of semantics that theologians love to discuss to give themselves some point of value or relevance.

Like most of the Hebrew prophets who preceded him John lived in very austere and frugal manner. He could be found on a daily basis going around promising justice and speaking out against those leaders he did not approve of. Of course one of these was Herod who he thought really should not have married the wife of his brother Philip. Just as nowadays, there are some people who do not accept criticism with grace and magnanimity and it has been suggested that Herod's wife seemed to be one of these people.

Following the long established traditions John used water in his rites of purification rite to assist repentant sinners in becoming better people which is a very nice thing to do. As a cat Little Kit was not overly fond of being dunked in water and so had tended to avoid this particular human malarkey.

Now, according to the Gospel of Luke both of John's parents were sterile, and in those days this made having children very difficult indeed. Luckily the angel Gabriel popped up as he often used to do back then presenting them with a good working solution to their difficulties. Perhaps it helped that both his mother and father were decedents of Aaron, as are most of the characters included in this story. John was only six months older than Jesus

According to funny old Flavius Josephus who is generally considered as being a bit more reliable than the wrings attributed to Luke, many Jews of the time thought that the destruction of Herod's army came as a just punishment from God for his part in the decapitation of his prophet, As you now Little Kit is often suspicious of such hopes of divine karma.

The Islamic perspective is much the same. In the Qur'an John the Baptist is known as Yohana in Arabic. It tells how his Father was not actually mute but that he did not speak for three nights when told that he was going to have a son who would carry on his work. Well, everyone likes to make a prophet! Apparently there are a number walking among the human race that still choose to believe that John the Baptist is the only true Messiah.

So we can see that the beheading was fairly unjustified and politically stupid. Perhaps there was a deeper meaning behind it all. Even though it seems a tad heretical Little Kit is starting to suspect that John might have actually wanted to have his head chopped off, but surely that would fly in the face of the laws of self preservation that govern us all?

29. Consider Prescience

Prescience fact: The so called Mayan Long Count colander that predicted the end of days was not the work of Mayans at all, but was the work of the Olmec people who Little Kit can exclusively reveal were actually from Africa even though no-one else seems to want to acknowledge this. Why do you think this is?

You will be pleased to know that we are well over half way through the telling of this little story. Most of the main characters have been introduced and many of the themes and elements that combined to allow Little Kit to eventually solve this puzzle. He hopes that you have found some pleasure in sharing his journey and that at least one or more of the matters he has discussed will have helped to stimulate you in a positive way.

In truth this had been quite a difficult time for Kit. He was one of those cats who tended to gloss over the problems he faced, but now he thinks it only fair that his situation has become increasingly difficult. Whilst the health of Little Kit the small black and white cat who was actually an ancient spirit who possessed the soul of a large old man was essentially quite good, the same could not be said of his host. The man who was now called Kit was deteriorating still further. It seems impossible that the health of a possessed man who has a virtual locked in state of being following vascular dementia and is blind and deaf and just sits all day unable to move or think could get any worse: but it has! Kit the man had a serious heart condition caused by ischemic heart failure. Basically his heart did not pump enough oxygen around his system. Also he had developed type two diabetes. This means his body no longer produced enough insulin to help his body manage the sugars that were in his body. Both of these conditions had been developing over recent years and gradually worsening. Usually both were manageable and the care staff could ensure his medication was taken regularly and the appropriate tests were properly conducted.

Sadly the way the world works does not always follow the exacting medical directions that consultants require. Kit the man had developed a bad sore in his foot and it was becoming very painful indeed. Kit the man had no possible way of explaining the pain he was in to his nurses and the situation was getting more and more desperate as each day went by. It was only by chance Little Kit the cat was in his soul and knew w=how bad the situation was becoming. Of course this is all a very heavy burden. Little Douggie Hiscox had always said "A problem shared is a blooming nuisance!" So it was Little Kit had been feeling pretty depressed and distressed lately and hoped that you will understand if this tale is not quite as jaunty as his usual efforts.

Anyway, the last thing Little Kit the cat wants to do is depress you with too many details of these events and so he wants to carry on with the telling of his tale. During his travels he was always interested to view the role of mystical pseudo sciences. Necromancy was a particular favourite of Little Kit. He had sometimes lived the life of a tarot card oracle and was pretty much a dab hand in the divination of dreams and the interpretation of wakefulness.

Necromancy is a practice of communication with those who have already died in order to discover hidden knowledge. It sounds a lot worse than it actually is. All around the world people are quite happy to say prayers to Holy memories; it is all a matter of perspective. The currently accepted view seems to be that necromancy was related to early forms of shamanism which called upon spirits such as the ghosts of ancestors. It was a practice adopted across the entire ancient world

As far back as the writing of the Book of Deuteronomy in the Bible you can read that the Israelites are warned against engaging in the exotic Canaanite practice of divination from the dead:
When thou art come into the land which the Lord thy God gives thee, thou shalt not learn to do according to

the abominations of those nations. There shall not be found among you any one who makes his son or his daughter to pass through the fire, or who uses divination, or an observer of times, or an enchanter, or a witch, or a charmer, or a consulter with familiar spirits, or a wizard, or a necromancer. For all who do these things are an abomination unto the Lord, and because of these abominations the Lord thy God doth drive them out from before thee.

Well the Israelites, like Little Kit, were not always best at following orders and so they often used to break the rules, even though the punishment in this case was the death penalty.

Given that Kit has lived many millions of lives he always found it quite nice when people used to call on him for his advice and potential knowledge of future events. To him it made good sense that his awareness should be a useful resource to those who followed. But then he was always being called a false prophet and so no-one really benefitted in the end. Still, he was always willing to try and assist if he could. Being polite was a significant part of his essential nature as you have already discovered.

Of course necromancy existed on Earth in all of the thousands and thousands of civilizations across the many universes that existed before the odd little one that you are currently enjoying. No-one likes to think that dead people are completely obsolete and useless do they? The whole business of human relics relies on the notion that there is some power that remains.

The modern view suggests that necromancy is a convoluted synthesis of astral magic which has been derived from older Arabic influences and exorcism derived from Gnostic Christian and Jewish teachings. The influence of the alchemists can be seen in the associated rituals that involve moon phases and the placement of the sun across the sky. Experiments conducted in the day were thought to be able to produce very different results from those conducted in the houses of night.

If you were to follow the trends of recent considerations you can easily see that practitioners of necromancy across all races have been the most highly revered of their various societies. Sometimes they were honoured and sometimes they were feared. Kit will not be the first person to suggest the theory that knowledge is a form of power and people are sometimes worried about things they do not fully understand. It is natural. It is thought that those who conducted these practices. Many possessed a basic knowledge of exorcism and some had access to texts demonology and astrology. Most were trained under apprenticeships and were expected to have a basic knowledge of declining or extinct base languages or runes, rituals and sacred hidden doctrines. In Kit's mind graveyards are monuments to the futility of human existence. They follow a tradition of unwavering pointlessness.

Necromancers liked to believe that they could create illusions of power and manipulate the will of others. Some were said to try and summon demons but this seems quite fanciful to the modern ways of viewing the world. It has been said that practitioners of the ancient arts would draw circles and pentagons on the floor and used occult symbols to augment their works. It was said that sacrifice was a key element to the rituals, but that all proved to be fodder for a different agenda to the one that was perceived by Little Kit. There are reasons why these practices have been given such a negative press and if you need to dig deeper then you might find the entire subject more user friendly than the usual perspective found in polite circles. It has always had a bad name and even our favourite renaissance man Leonardo da Vinci wrote:

"Of all human opinions that is to be reputed the most foolish are those that deal with the belief in necromancy, the sister of alchemy, which gives birth to simple and natural things."

There has always been a fear among those who do not comprehend dark matters. For some strange reason sorcery in all its many forms seems to have evoked a universal bad press from the offset.

30. Consider Packaging

Packaging Fact: You have nineteen million skin cells for each square inch of your body.

You might remember that the small crude box that contained the bright red head of John the Baptist that was found in the shed at the bottom of the garden was made from gopher wood. For those of you interested in such things might remember that God himself expected Noah to make his ark out of gopher wood, and this was something of a problem as there is no such thing as a gopher tree. As you can imagine the great minds of history have been thinking very carefully about this particular irrelevant conundrum, as they are want to do, and have come up with some interesting suggestions.

There have been lots of alternative trees suggested the most popular one seems to be cedar wood. Anyone who actually like reading about Little Kit will almost certainly be thinking of the singing Cedars of Anastasia at this point, but that would be one of those deflections he tries so hard to avoid. There were suggestions that it was actually the wood from the Cyprus tree that was used. Meanwhile other people have mooted particular favourites ranging from ebony and juniper through to simple rushes and wickerwork. There have been arguments proposing pine and teak whilst others prefer to consider the merits of boxwood and acacia wood.

One Greek chap translated gopher to mean any squared timber, but we all know that translators can change anything into something else more easily than an alchemist can. A couple of centuries later Latin Vulgate Bible, said by some to be the oldest known bible, seems to say that the word meant simply planed wood. Some people have said that gopher wood is made up with heavily slimed river rushes and others say it is a general term that can related to any resinous type of wood. Another idea is that it was a term that described any wood that was covered with pitch to make it seaworthy. So Little Kit wonders why it is that God chose to instruct Noah to build a vessel that would save all of creation from a substance that no-one had ever heard of? He would say that it all seems a wee bit "cabbagey"!

As you will have imagined, the pointless arguments continued. There is a more modern view that says the gopher tree did exist in its own right as a perfectly functioning separate tree species growing happily in the places where trees like to live but it has somehow been lost to us, a victim of extinction. Little Kit likes to think that there is somewhere hidden from the mainstream world where an ancestor of this long forgotten tree still thrives in secret. Perhaps we are thinking of a place similar to the island of Socotra? Who knows? It will remain one of the lesser mysteries of the universe until some bright expert comes along and proves otherwise, only to be replaced by a newer and brighter expert in the fullness of time, because, to cats, this seems to be how experts work.

Relics have always been jolly important items and people may pay a lot of money for a decent part of something that might once have been considered as important. Let's think about this for a moment. How much would you pay for a small plank of wood that came directly from Noah's Ark? It would probably be worth more than what you would pay from a small plank that came from the Golden Hind, or from the Endeavour or even from the Titanic. There is big money to be made from selling useless bits of old wood, and humans like nothing more than having big money. Now Phillip the Tetrarch, remember him, the uncle of Salome and former husband of Queen Herodias Was a man who had quite a lot of money and a particular interest in certain religious and mystical matters. He was one of those people who could be persuaded to spend a fortune on a genuine item of immense potential power.

So there he was very happy that he had this most precious of holy artefacts when he came into possession of the head of John the Baptist. At this point Philip the

Tetrarch considered himself to be the luckiest man on Earth. He owned the greatest treasure of the day.

To understand why the head of John the Baptist was so important to Phillip you need to think like a ruler of a small tribe of people based around Palestine at a time when Romans were wandering around conquering things and all the people were pretty depressed and reliant on whatever religion they followed. It was not always easy. Because he was wiser and more experienced in arcane practices he was one of the few people around who know that the head of John the Baptist was a reciprocal for the Holy Spirit and all that implied.

Pharouk was the sort of chap who kept his own counsel. He was quiet at the best of times and because of the scars on his face it was hard to read his expressions. People did not like looking directly at him anyway. He was on his annual caravan journey heading north when he called into the palace at Caeserea Philippi to see he favourite customer Philip the Alchemist. It was just the usual materials this time, sulphur and mercury and various types of quartz and resins. In previous years Philip had requested various exotic and rare items and Pharouk had always tried to oblige. So this particular year Pharouk was not particularly surprised when he was asked if he might be able to arrange a delivery of some gopher wood in the next couple of months. Although it really was an exceedingly rare commodity Pharouk did know of a source that had a treasured plank of wood that had originally been recovered from Mount Ararat. Of course, it would be incredibly expensive, but Pharouk was certain a deal could be done. Pharouk knew that a deal could always be done.

So an order was placed and Pharouk was given a maximum budget and the order was placed. Of course at no point did he ask what Philip wanted the gopher wood for, that was none of his business and as something of an alchemist himself he knew the importance of keeping secrets. It was a pleasant exchange as Philip and his master were always good and generous hosts. Over dinner that night Philip asked Pharouk if he knew of an excellent carpenter who he could commission to create a really special case for a particular artefact. Well Pharouk had travelled around a lot and said that there was this one carpenter who used to live in Nazareth but was now spending his time as a wondering preacher over by Galilee who he had always been very impressed by. As it happens Philip the Alchemist had heard of this chap who had actually visited the city a couple of years earlier on his way up Mount Herman. He thanked Pharouk and said that was useful information that he would certainly follow up. As we now know Pharouk was able to negotiate a fair price for the plank of gopher wood and arranged for it to be delivered over to Philip. It really was quite remarkable how many good contacts he had that had helped him establish such a well respected business.

31, Consider Popeye

Popeye fact: Popeye was not always a spinach fanatic. In early stories the sailor-man gained his special powers by rubbing the head of a magical Whiffle Hen with the unlikely name Bernice.

Little Douggie Hiscox had a strange sense of déjà vu. It was at a time of impossibility as so many visions tend to be. He was standing on board the half sail and half steam ship that was run by his great grandmother. It was not as unusual for Welsh women at that time to be a pirate as you might think. The Penula was a sturdy enough boat that had managed the trip across to Egypt and backs to Aberaeron a couple of time. Her son Captain Twm was happily settled in more legal endeavours running a small collage in Aberaeron to help teach budding sailors how to be captains. The land was in their blood but the sea was in their hearts. It was often the way for those whose roots were firmly based in the South of Carmarthenshire a few hundred years ago, It was not that The Penula was particularly feared, but the crew were enterprising, that is how the declining world of piracy was moving. Nowadays the pirates operating off the shores of Socotra and other places have to contend with better equipped shipping filled with guards who have better firearms, so they need even more speed and cunning than those hardy Welsh women who were cutting their own path through history. At home it was possible to live off the spoils of wrecking, but that was fraught with obvious dangers and was deemed as being somewhat more unworthy.

Anyway, the Penula was caught in a particularly heavy storm in the Bay of Naples and was about to be taking her last short journey in a southerly direction. The winds were deafening, the water slashing across

161

the bows was unrelenting and all those on board were aware of their inevitable and immediate demise. It was a time to take stock and evaluate the value and purpose of each person's experience. The Captain was feeling proud of her achievements but was upset the entire crew were about to die. It was her responsibility to get the ship home safely, but that was not going to happen. Two of the crew were sad that they were going to drown quite so far away from home; the other two were glad that their ending would not be a burden on anyone else.

Because he was from more modern times Little Douggie Hiscox was quite aware that he had a very different perspective on affairs. He did not have the certainty of a religion to bolster him at this stressful time. He did not have the understanding of a life at sea where this sort of misadventure is a daily possibility. He was not as well equipped for death as this great grandmother, and he knew that, had it not have been just a dream, he would have been dissatisfied if this was how everything was to end. It was quite a romantic sort of finale, but still nasty, brutish and short when everything else is taken into account. As the ship began to break up and the huge dirty waters come raging up to devour their pray he was aware of a strange smell across the starboard bow. For a split second it reminded him of the raw cabbages he used to pick from his grandfathers allotment. And then it was all gone. He woke up and wondered what on Earth all that had meant. Then he went off to work and forgot it had ever happened. This seems to be how our shared journey works.

So we move away from that crisis and move to another. It can easily observable that there have been times when it has been pretty difficult to be Jewish. Certainly the Iberian Peninsula and its environs were not the best place for the Mendoza's and Pallache families at the times of the Inquisition and various other centuries around it. Anti Semitism seems such a strange notion to a politically tolerant black and white cat. Yet people often believe in the evil that is thrown at others and such labels can permeate generations. It was hard enough for Samuel Pallache to grow up in Fez being despised for the religion he was born into. His father was a rabbi and his uncle was actually venerated as the Great rabbi of Fez. Traditions and honour had always been drilled into him. He tried to assimilate and be useful to the Sultan of Morocco and was slowly starting to be more accepted. However, in his hear he knew this would never be.

Samuel had absolutely no interest in alchemy at all. However he was erroneously considered to be realisable and trustworthy and so was given the opportunity to become one of the team of guardians to the caves that held the secret treasures of the "Keepers of Aaon's Promise". At this point the very last thing on his mind was that he would become a thief. It really was just the very strangest thing. When he thought about it afterwards he just could not explain what it was that happened. He was just doing his job as dutifully as he could, as proud as it was possible to be that he was helping to improve the perception of his family and his people. Suddenly from out of absolutely no-where an overwhelming desire came over him to secretly pick up an old wooden box in the corner of the

163

cave and take it home with him. It was the weirdest compulsion and after that everything changed.

Following this Samuel no longer felt that he was reliable or could be trusted. Within weeks he had become increasingly calculating and starting to take ever bigger and bigger risks. His ambition was starting to be noticed and from being a quiet and meek soul he started to emerge with greater confidence. As he attracted increasing attention so the Sultan decided that this was a man who could be sent out into the wider world to delegate with the many factions across the area that were demanding his attention. So it was that just one small moment of seeming madness set him on a path that caused him to become the associate of the great and mighty.

As a diplomat and trader Pallache fell very quickly foul of the anti-Jewish sentiments when all the Protestant pastors successfully protested from allowing him to settle in the Netherlands. However a number of years later Sultan of Morocco appointed him to be his agent in The Hague. He was involved in helping to forge an alliance against Spain. However all was not what is seemed as Samuel was actually a double agent who passed information to both the Spanish and Dutch/Moroccan sides. He was also a pirate and a privateer who just seemed to be able to survive more powerfully from whatever awful scrape he found himself facing.

Oddly, before he started travelling around Europe and even the New World he found that he had suddenly started "speaking in tongues". It was all very disconcerting. Of all the gifts he could have been given why did it have to be that one?

32. Consider Problem Solving

Problems solving fact: All detectives will have clearly defined skills in problem solving including the use of creative and abstract thought processes. Little Kit considered himself to be quite good at it.

The trouble was that the box that Jesus had made was simply too small. You could look at it another way and say that the head was too big. It was not his fault, for he was without sin, it was all down to the fact that the amount of wood in the gopher wood plank was not enough to create a container any larger than the one that had been produced. There are fundamental neo-scientific laws of the universe that control such things and in Palestine in around the year 32 AD this was a common feature of the predominant culture.

Now both Philip the Tetrarch and Philip the Alchemist were practical sort of men. They knew that he was unlikely to be able to get any more gopher wood to make the box bigger and so that left them with the less favoured option of trying to somehow get the head of John the Baptist a bit smaller so that it could fit into the space that the carpenter had unknowingly made for it.

So the first thing they considered was splitting the head down the back and pulling out some of the brains and innards and somehow making it fit that way. Yet, what if they tried that and the Holy Spirit that was inside the head managed to escape, that would be unthinkable! Of course they could shave all that shaggy ridiculous hair off, but that was something of a trademark of the Baptist and might cause displeasure to God, which was the last thing they wanted. It certainly was a very great predicament and so they did what people usually do when facing a very difficult problem. They took the easy way out.

They called for the wild trader Pharouk to see if he could offer any sage advice. Over the years of their various dealings both of the two Philip's had come to realise that Pharouk was a man of very many hidden talents and strange elemental knowledge. There was no-one in his current court that they could trust with this delicate and potentially expensive and explosive conundrum.

So it was one morning in late February that the scruffy disfigured trader shuffled his unloved form into the City to discover the reason why his presence had been requested. Traders are used to unexpected summoning; it was an occupational reality. Usually the messenger would give him clear instructions requiring him to bring a specific substance or at least a clue into what situation he was encountering. So a simple request just to see Philip who was asking for advice on an unspecified subject was actually quite an alluring prospect. Pharouk had been so badly treated as a child that he actually loved the idea that nowadays Kings were calling for his attention. He allowed himself a smile of satisfaction to think that a scar-faced dark-skinned exile from the remote island of Socotra could have travelled so far in the years since he was an outcast teen.

Pharouk was wise enough to know that his very presence in the royal court was of itself a major event in the normally routine world of such places. The court officials and standing soldiers would spend hours in discussions and speculation over the coming days trying to divine why it might be that their wonderful and powerful King might want to speak to this pathetic shabby disfigured foreigner.

They would never know. Pharouk played his enigmatic role as well as always in his time fashioned way. His haltering shuffle was perhaps a little bit more pronounced than it needed to be. He grinned and startled gazing crazily from his one good eye flashing around to maximise its impact on those with more perfect physiologies. He was a very wealthy man who could easily ensure his robes were always clean, but it helped his performance to look the part of a helpless itinerant. He was usually accompanied by hired brutes to stave off any unwanted attention, but when it came to the final part of his entry to meet the King he decided it would be safe enough to approach unaccompanied.

Phillip the Tetrarch too had dismissed all of his usual retinue. The two men settled cross legged on a bright carpet in the tent that had been prepared and there was no-one present to overhear their conversation. The guards at the entrance to the tent were well out of earshot and so the matter at hand could be considered in strictest confidence, This too was quite rare for the times, usually those of a lower rank were deemed as invisible and many a secret proved not to be a secret at all due to this simple and obvious oversight. It was true then, it is perhaps even truer nowadays.

Phillip informed Pharouk of the problem he had in managing his two main treasures. Either the head of John the Baptist was too big or the gopher box was too small. How could this situation be reconciled?

Pharouk could immediately think of a solution. It had been an excellent decision to seek out his advice because he knew of a method where the integrity of both objects could be fully maintained and the unification of sacred items made even more spectacular. This was exactly what Phillip wanted to hear, but he was amazed by what the ugly little trader was proposing.

During his time in Egypt the shabby looking trader Pharouk had clandestine dealings with a number of different sages who were seeking to discover the "Elixir of Life". It was just one of those things that happened to be a pretty big deal among the overeducated idle rich of the Kingdom. He would often be sent to various locations all across the Middle East to gather certain specific valued items from the many, many connections he had made trough his trading endeavours. It was nothing for him to be sent to travel a thousand miles simply to get some specific type of mineral or wood or potion or scent. That was the role of the trader and he was regarded as the best trader around.

Pharouk was himself a master of the arcane and mystic arts and he knew many others who were even more proficient than he was. As a trader he was aware of all the key components to the hidden arts and was more aware of their specific ingredients and requests than anyone else. He probably knew more about their various triumphs and failures than any other person.

He had a pretty good idea about who was good at certain things and who was good at other things, Of course, he knew a man who might be good at either making a box bigger but using no more wood, or who might be able to make a head smaller, but not damage it in any way. That man Pharouk himself.

The mummification and preservation of bodies in his adopted land was legendary and he was well aware of how to enlarge and shrink a head and leave it in a perfect condition. It was simply the use of hot stones and key ingredients and rituals at the time of a gibbous moon. It was as simple as dimple really. He was able to complete the task within days as the season of the moon was favourable. That was another task successfully completed and Pharouk was pleased that he had been able to assist such important customers. You will appreciate that Phillip was ecstatically pleased to learn that his problem had been solved. The relic was intact and the power of the Holy Spirit remained intact now safely housed in its tight fitting wooden container. Philip the Tetrarch went to his royal bed that night thinking to himself that life just does not get any better.

33. Consider Pugnance

Pugnance fact: What do you think will be the punishment for those who decided to call a roller coaster ride after her when Nemesis, the Greek goddess of divine retribution, finds out what they have done?

Now do you remember at the start of this story the writer told you that Little Kit had a nemesis that was called Pugnance? This would normally be the point where we start to give more serious consideration to the role that she played in this particular adventure. However, there is not really too much to talk about. In many of his previous journeys Pugnance had been following him around like an unwanted shadow trying to disrupt what it was he was seeking to achieve. Yet on this journey following the "Path of Melancholy" it seemed as if Pugnance did not really want to get involved. Now Little Kit was suspicious by nature and he knew there must be a reason why this was, but he had yet to discover exactly what the cause of this reluctance might be.

Like Little Kit, Pugnance was an ancient soul who had been travelling though her own journeys. At some point their paths had crossed, he thought these were a deliberate attempt by her to cause him botheration, although she would always try to assure him that is was mere coincidence. Well we all know that Kit does not hold much regard for that particular explanation. Neither knew it, but most of the other ancient souls used to laugh at their relationship, some thought they must be Brother and Sister, others thought they were potential lovers who have yet to find the right circumstances. Kit would not have been impressed by these suggestions, to him Pugnance was just a nuisance who used to interfere with his various attempts to help whichever host he happened to be residing in.

Now you will probably have a view of the world and time that suggests this is the only evolution of time and the universe and all the atoms and vibrations that currently surround us. It is a fair enough point of view to hold given the limitations that humans need to exist by. Those who come from more ancient times will hold a totally different point of reference. They understand that there have been millions and millions of incarnations of Earth and all the planets and the heavens and all life forms and non-life forms.

Kit could not really remember the first time their paths crossed, all he remembered was a feeling of annoyance whenever he heard her name or was reminded that she existed. The ancient souls were not a particularly social race and tended to try and avoid each other in the intricate weavings of the universe they happen to be residing in. For some reason he associated her with Ganymede, but that was just a glancing memory, nothing he could actually articulate. Anyway, there were quite a few of the ancient souls hanging around in Palestine and Egypt at the time of Herod the Great. Anytime there was an intervention by Angels in the lives of men there seemed to be some magnetic attraction that drew the older ones to survey whatever would emerge from the inevitable confusion that would arise. You don't need to be a theological expert to understand that such occasions are fraught with errors and miscommunication.

In earlier days Pugnance had been a truly great alchemist. She had been involved in helping to create the "Emerald Tablet" the earliest of all the arcane records which had helped establish the art in ancient Egypt. She was the one who had started the obsession with discovering the formula for the "Elixir of Life". Kit had know that her aims had started off quite honourably and that it was her intention that the studies would encourage spiritual awakenings and generate blessings of a more profane nature. It was not

171

her fault that mankind is vulgar by nature and cannot help itself from turning those things that are golden into something that is base. By their very design it seems that humans are alchemists in reverse.

Kit was fully aware that Pugnance had wanted to promote purity and beauty and seek the pursuit of perfection and harmony. Little did she know the entire process would end up with grubby little men in grubby little holes desperately seeking out gold that they did not deserve? It should not come as a great surprise for you to learn that the journey taken by the box containing the head of John the Baptist roughly follows the pathway of the teachings of alchemy in the western world. Starting in Egypt through Arabia, a dalliance with the Greeks and then the Romans before being further progressed in Spain and then into Amsterdam and into England. Well, there are a great many things that follow the pathway of great civilizations, perhaps that is an inevitable by-product of latent power? This mirrored the journey taken by Pugnance before she ended up as a spirit possessing the soul of a bemused black cat somewhere down a dead end path in a forsaken corner of Cardiff.

For herself Pugnance had always been very fond of Little Kit. When she had promised the "First Ones" that she would keep an eye out for the runt of the ancient soul litter she had not realised that it would have been such a vast undertaking. It had not always been easy to keep a discrete distance when she observed all the different scrapes her small charge managed to get into. Most times Little Kit had been unaware of her presence as she had followed his progress across the eons. Quite recently she had occasionally possessed

Aunty Tilly just to make sure that Little Kit was not endangering the space-time continuum or troubling the hiding angels. Most of the time she did not regret her offer of assistance; it had usually been quite entertaining. The other ancient souls could be quite cutting about his eccentricities and lack of discipline and she had always been able to defend him. Pugnance had realised very early on that this was a truly thankless task.

34. Consider Popping Back

Popping back fact: People following the traditions of Hinduism may sometimes hit the head of dead people as they believe that the soul needs to be freed from the memories of the body.

There is a school of thought that suggests that resurrection is just reincarnation done in a speedy sort of way. Now all over the world there are millions of people who quite definitely are of the view that reincarnation is as much a reality as life itself, so it is not a concept to be simply dismissed. So to help this story reach a point where you might want to focus on this, because it partly relates to the thinking that guided Phillip the Tetrarch to request the head of John the Baptist in the first place. In simple terms Phillip wanted to live forever. In his court he had many sages and philosophers and a handful of alchemists, the most prominent of which was also called Philip. Little Kit is hoping that will not be too confusing for those who are reading this story.

In itself the quest for immortality is not an uncommon ambition. As a consequence he had spent most of his adult life using his spare time to study all aspects of endeavour to see how this might be achieved. Remember, he was brought up on the fringes of a society where Egyptians seemed happily to send their Kings off into immortality. He wanted all of that, but he wanted it so that he could stay on Earth and maintain his role of being a ruling King here too. There were lots of stories about people who overcame death, it was not just Lazarus, and they all needed to be considered and were discussed widely in the houses of those who held power.

There were many people who have shared this particular goal across time. As a recent example, when the idea for the film Jurassic Park was pitched it fully resonated with the general public. By and large people liked the idea of being able to rekindle the DNA of an extinct animal and bring it back to life. It is based on potential truth as scientists have found that when small insects trapped in amber are freed after over ten thousand years they can show signs of life. Other scientists have discovered that worms trapped in permafrost in Siberia will start wriggling again after seventy thousand years of stillness. It is a miracle. Of course, the reality is that this sort of thing happens millions of times all over the plant in ways humans do not yet understand. There are trillions of virus forms and bacteria floating around today who were not here yesterday but were certainly here at the time the continents we now have were currently formed. There are creatures from pre-history dancing all around you and within you and you have no notion at all that they exist. Just as they have no idea that you exist either. It is a pretty good system. So in all the places on the globe where glaciers crash into the sea there will always be old life forms coming back to say hello. This happens every second of every moment. In those areas where the heat of the land warms the earth there is almost a certainty of refreshment. It is likely that human endeavour will result in the return of the ever popular sabre-tooth tiger and the mammoth. Who knows where it will end? Perhaps you will be able to order your Granny back via an illegal online trading service, there is really no reason why this will not happen. In fact, it is quite likely that, for the wealthier and more privileged among you that it will.

Now this is where the search for the "Fountain of Youth" moves to centre stage. As you have determined this "Elixir of Life" is believed to provide perfection and immortality and often equated with the item they treasured the most, the "Philosopher's Stone". This potion is said to grant the drinker the gift of eternal youth and has been searched for all across the globe. For the purposes of this small story Little Kit has largely taken the reader through the alchemists associated in the West. He would strongly encourage those who are interested in such matters to consider the other sources available

As just a tiny sweetener for what you might find he can tell you that his old friends in China firmly believed that eating long lasting precious substances like hematite, cinnabar and green jade in the belief some of their perceived longevity would pass into the person who consumed them. If ever you were invited for dinner over there you needed to keep your eyes wide open. Now if you too have the mind of a detective you might want to look into the way Kit solved the cases of three thousand missing children, but that belongs to another story at another time. The search for "amrita" in India has been a worthy quest for many. Then there are the ancient rituals of those cultures of South America, North America, Australasia, mainland Africa and Northern Europe that all help to shape our collective awareness of the profane and sacred past. Yes indeed, perfection is certainly hard to discover.

Still all of this is a glorious distraction. It is almost as if there is an invisible force trying to stop Little Kit from completing this simple tale. Going back to the thread of our story; like most of the clever people living in The Levant in those days Philip the Alchemist firmly believed that the spirit of God equated to the miracle that encapsulated the immorality and beauty that the "Elixir of Life" could provide. It would prevent him from ever being ill for all of eternity. He knew that somehow John the Baptist had the ability to channel the Holy Spirit and he firmly believed that he would be able to access this power too. It was not just for himself. Aside from all the various other warring factions that historically had bothered his clan the Romans had come along and he would like to change that particular political dynamic. Surly his motives were pure enough?

35. Consider Pit Workers

Pit workers fact: The death of coal mining. In 1920 there were over 1,191,000 people in the coal industry in Great

Britain. Just one hundred years later there are less than two thousand. Everything must die and then must die again, and again. This is how it all works!

There are a lot of deaths that can be considered as unfortunate for a whole host of different reasons. For example we see epidemics of various illnesses, ships sinking, mighty storms and lots of mines collapsing. Death will come to visit us all despite the best efforts of all the alchemists that have ever existed.

The death of Douggie Hiscox was particularly vexing for his family. He could no longer be considered as little and no-one had used that name since he stopped boxing some fifty years earlier. He had been found completely dead at his home having silently slipped into the forever darkness of his final destination. Whilst it was sad in some ways as he was a lovely person. What made it particularly vexatious for his family was the very last thing he did. On checking is desk there was a message to his son on a notepad that simply said "David, after all these years of keeping this as a secret it is vitally important that I tell you t........" The message was never completed.

So what was it that he was going to say? No-one would ever really know. Of course, people speculated, that is the sort of thing that happens in events like this. Inevitably there was a coroner's inquest; nowadays there has to bc onc at cvery single incident of sudden and unexplained death. They could point to some possible physical factors that might have has an impact on his health. For instance he had various bullet wounds in his legs when he had been shot quite intentionally by the Japanese and quite unintentionally by the Americans during his time of service in Burma. It was evident that he had contracted malaria whilst there too and this had generally weakened his system. Of course he had smoked heavily throughout his life and had been raised in a mining community where the very air was filled with coal. He had emphysema and asthma as well as bronchitis and had been wrongly treated for each, so that had not been helpful and his lungs were in poor condition. He had suffered with gout and stomach problems and intermittent arthritis along with all the usual health concerns that effected people who were born in 1920. However his actual cause of death was cited as cancer. All those millions and millions of strange little cells wreaking the havoc they were created to do. There were minor bruises arising from the fall and general grazes arising, but no actual blood was left at the scene. All this was very interesting to the few people around who might have wished to know. The process of analysing his actual cause of death was all very thorough and professional. However, what it failed to answer was the key question that everyone really wanted to know. What on Earth was the great secret that Doug Hiscox, as he was then known, had to tell?

Now you will have realised that in his essence Little Kit the black and white cat is something of a detective. To prove it he will now tell you something about you. For example are you male or female? Well twenty year ago this would have been pretty easy and. Without wishing to be accused of sexism Little Kit would contend that women generally did not read stories like this, only teenage boys, but now we live in more flexible times. So he is not going to commit himself to that.

What he will say with a greater level of certainty is that you are privileged and that you probably do not realise it. Of course, all these things are relative but in many areas of the world having the time and resources and ability to read a book rely on a huge range of background factors ranging from political stability through to access to education. Most people who have got these do not appreciate how valuable they are. It is pretty straightforward really.

It is likely that you did not buy this book yourself. It is amazing, how does a small cat who has never even met you or knows who you are know this about you? He is good isn't he? So what age are you? Again this is a moving figure; twenty years ago you would have been likely to have been under thirty, now any reader of this would probably be aged over thirty. It is all part of the way the world sweeps in cycles, nothing to do with you at all.

What else can he say about you? Well it is likely that you do not follow any particular belief system and that you value the certainty that your society places upon science. Everything that takes you away from modern thinking you tend to dismiss as rubbish in your mind, although you might not actually say this to anyone else who you thought might have more sympathetic views on spiritual issues. This is not to say that you are not a spiritual person, but that you are not inclined to accept the certainty of any particular religion, just as most of the people around you no longer have a strict faith in the traditional sense. Then Kit would say that you personally have a stronger determination than many others. It is pretty clear that a disjointed story like this will not suit most tastes and so if you have stuck it out thus far it says quite a lot about your personality, don't you think? Then there is the content matter itself.

Most people would not be remotely interested in the strange ranting of a half-man half-cat suffering from dementia, but here we are, a significant way though this process and you have tried your best to stick with it. Then there is the question of the fundamental purpose of the story, is it a detective story, or a love story or a horror, what genre does it fall into and are you the kind of person who generally is interested in these types of things. Well the answer strangely is a resounding 'no'! You are not at all interested in the kinds of things this book talks about and would not normally have more than a mild interest in the properties of resins of unusual plants or the convoluted descriptions of a cabbage.

Kit would contend that all these factors suggest that you are actually quite a nice person. You may have some negative thoughts about things from time to time but essentially you do not wish to harm any other creature and are the kind of person who would be happy to stroke a cat. Not that Kit liked being stroked, but he likes the fact that you are more likely to be nice to him than not.

Now then, all of that is pretty straightforward so now let's be a wee bit more specific. Little Kit knows that you have a secret and that you intend to keep this deep dark secret deep within you until the day you die. You know that it will affect other people if ever this secret is revealed. Well Little Kit is a great believer in keeping secrets. Of course, being a detective he sees it as his job to reveal secrets, but not at the cost of causing any harm to anyone. It is not that he is overburdened by morality, or even that he actually cares about such things, but he just follows the universal code of seeking to cause the least harm. Remember there are many small birds and mice who have been cruelly taunted that would say cats do not have an overwhelming sense of kindness. Let's face it; the universe is sometimes a bit hard to fully understand.

Politically you are moribund. You are fully aware that you are being constantly lied to and misdirected by all media outlets but have decided to accept this position because it is comfortable for you to do so. You know that there is a major famine somewhere, there is always a famine somewhere, but that is just something that you cannot change. There are arms being sold by people in your country and that is not something you would approve of, but it is still happening and will continue to take place. You like to think that you do not benefit from this and would not like a small black and white cat telling you something different. Well, who would? We have accepted that you are comfortable and complacent, Face facts; you are not going to wake up tomorrow and pack a bag and hitch-hike away to Nepal. It is a fanciful idea, but you have commitments and where would we be if everyone just decided to act on such whims? Nepal would be full of people worrying about what was going on at home.

Of yes, you have a particularly fine sense of humour and irony. You really would not have made it this far into the book if you were not able to feel amused by the world around you and the role that you have been given to fulfil.

You are a child of your age. You have no interest at all in whatever it is the Holy Ghost is or does because you do not perceive this as being a matter of importance to you. You have no real fear of eternal damnation even though it was a prime moving daily factor for your great grandparents and all the generations that made you before them. You cannot really understand why there are acts of brutality in the world. The beheadings of various peoples around the world cannot be explained to you in any way that would make you sympathetic to their perpetrators. Things like the human sacrifice of children practiced by various cults in the past are so completely alien to your way of thinking that they cause you more reprehension. You cannot forgive people killing children in the name of their particular cause, whatever it might be, because you firmly believe that murder is a bad thing and it is worse if it involves a child victim rather than an adult. In your head you think that all stories about possessions and demons and angels and ghosts and spirits are all utter nonsense, but may be based on some primal understanding related to the need to explain existence. You will firmly believe in the premise of evolution as it is currently understood and that science will always out master aspects of belief, which you perceive as mainly superstitious even though you like to feel that you have an open mind about such things.

You do not think that you have significance enough to change the status quo and that things will largely remain safe and secure in your world. You believe that there will probably be some hiccups along the way but essentially the future will be a better place. You absolutely hold the view that the present is better than the past. However, you also really do believe that there are some old traditions or areas of knowledge that have been forgotten or that are no longer practiced that would be interesting to know more about.

Despite all the evidence to the contrary you probably still think that the news that you are told on the television is the truth and cannot really see any reason why there might be some universal agenda behind what is presented. You know that you are essentially a nice person and that it would be quite important for you to believe that those who know you will also consider you to be basically one on the good guys.

You have developed your own strong set of morals and principles and have a genuine desire to uphold kindness and goodness and understanding, even though you would certainly not express this in those sorts of terms. The notion of love underpins what you have experienced. You have sought love and found a form of love and those sentiments are a core part of your feelings towards the world. You like music. You find nature to be wonderful and find animals really fascinating and wonderful. You still feel there is mystery in the world and have serious concerns that the progress science is bringing is not always in the best interests of the wider environment in which humans live.

Now we come to some more interesting aspects. You firmly believe that you are a free spirit who is able to make conscious decisions without being controlled by anyone else. You absolutely and firmly believe to your core that you are in complete control of your destiny and of your actions. You would totally reject any suggestion that you are in fact utterly controlled and have no real say in what happens to you.

Do you remember earlier in the book Little Kit made you aware that you are made up of only ten percent of human cells and ninety percent of other cells? This is a fact, look it up if you need to. So what have you done with this information? How has an awareness that you have over four pounds of bacteria alone living in you as a full part of what you are effected you? You have done nothing. What else could you do? However, when a small cat tells you that this is part of the programme that you have been issued with, then you should feel a bit cheated.

It is not your fault. It is all part of what the ancient ones have dubbed "The Great Lie". We all kid ourselves every single moment of every single day. You like to believe that you would like to know the truth. However, the truth is that you actually do not want to know the truth. The truth is that you have been programmed and that you are not in control and that the entire world is part of a far more subtle conspiracy that you and everyone else can never possibly understand. You are just bacteria on a cabbage. You know this is utterly true and in five minutes time you will be drinking tea and you have forgotten that you have been told this. Don't worry, that is just the way it has to be.

You still think that most people around you approximately see the world the world in roughly the same way that you do. What on Earth do you think tiny, humble bacteria can do that could possibly change a cabbage; and why would it even want to? Perhaps the cabbage is not so bad? There are lot worse things to be attached to than a green leafy vegetable, don't you think?

36. Consider Principles of Beheading

Principles of beheading fact: There are a number of animals, for example cockroaches, that can survive decapitation as they expire not directly from loss of their head, but instead due to starvation

Do you remember earlier on we discussed Alabast, the chap who was ordered to chop off the head of John the Baptist, never spoke of the matter again? Well the whole thing was so upsetting for him that he actually became less and less civil and in the end hardly ever spoke about anything at all. You see the act of beheading someone has a significant mental impact on the person who is doing the actual deed. The brutal act of severing takes a strange toll.

We just established that you personally are not really a great fan of beheading. Even if someone had kidnapped you and kept you locked in a caller and raped you repeatedly on a daily basis for two years you almost certainly would not have the constitution to actually behead someone yourself. There is a part of you that would be extraordinarily grumpy and probably would be more mindful to the possibility of someone else doing it, but even then it would not be a worldview that would sit particularly comfortably with you. However, there is someone being beheaded somewhere in the world today, just as there is every day. Now this might be because they have been considered to have done a very bad thing. It might be because they happen to believe something or even that they do not actually believe something that someone who has captured them happens to think. Nowadays it is less likely to be because the people undertaking the beheading believes that they will actually gain some benefit from chopping off someone's head, but that has not always been the case.

So what do you think might be the benefits that some people might hope for in the act of decapitation of someone else? Well, when you study this more deeply you will probably be surprised to discover that there are actually lots and lots of potential good reasons for this seemingly barbaric act.

Now the first thing to consider is that it is not a modern phenomenon, very little actually is. Beheading has been a pretty common sort of activity for millions and millions of years. There is a relic called the Namer Palette on permanent display at the entrance lobby Cairo Museum which had been dated back over five thousand year which features the decapitation of corpses. Most experts say it shows the killing of a King of Egypt at a time of the unification of the country. Other experts say it does not represent an actual event at all but is symbolic. So which expert do you choose to believe? Little Kit is always finding situations like this vexatious...

Nowadays we tend to think of beheading as being a jolly bad thing but this was not always the case. In ancient Rome and Greece, decapitation was regarded an honourable form of death. They had a number of significantly less appealing options to consider. If the executioners axe or sword was nice and sharp and the aim of the swing was precise then decapitation was quite quick and was presumed to be a relatively painless form of death. If the instrument was blunt or the headsman was clumsy, multiple strokes might be required to sever the head, resulting in a prolonged and more painful death. The person to be executed was therefore advised to pay the headsman in gold to ensure that he did his job with care. If John the Baptist had handed over any money to Alabast at the appointed time then Little Kit was not aware of it. History seems to suggest that beheadings are largely the province of men and women are rarely mentioned in such matters. Little Kit would suggest that the truth of this might not coincide entirely with the normally presented facts.

Of course the loss of a head is pretty symbolic in all sorts if other ways aside from the simple act of human decapitation. There are many types of flowers that you need to "dead head" in order to get better blooms the next time around. It certainly is a matter that might warrant further consideration. However, at this point Little Kit is aware that he is coming to a few elements where even the most avid reader might get bogged down and he does not want to interrupt the flow of this story more than is really necessary. He is thoughtful like that as any well brought up small black and white cat should be.

Kit had always felt quite fortunate when considering the way his brain works. Of course nowadays it is full of problems arising from his inherited organic brain failure. That is a genuine setback that comes with the onset of vascular dementia. He did not stop thinking clearly immediately; it had just got worse and worse with every passing week. He still likes to think he has held things together pretty well in his telling of this particular adventure. Hopefully any reader will not be too confused, and if you have been then you will probably not have made it this far into the story.

It all seems quite a long time ago now that Little Kit materialised into existence. Like most of us, he started off sometime after the very beginning of time itself, even though we have established such a place has never existed. We went through the arrival of the ancient souls who have always been here and of parasites and bacteria. Then we jumped a bit to the movement of continents and the strange plants that were separated by the forces that moved entire continents then we arrived at the giants who Kit wished he had not mentioned: no one likes talking about them anymore. It was then a simple procession of people and events that has brought the box holding the shrunken red head of John the Baptist to the place where we now are. It is all as simple as dimple!

Now we come to a very strange concept altogether. Be warned, it is not a consideration that will sit comfortably with your current rational view of the world,

37. Consider Purposes of the Holy Spirit

Purpose of the Holy Spirit Fact: You might be confused if you relied on the Bible to explain the role of the Holy Spirit as it says a few different things. Jesus is jolly

positive and notes kind things like the Spirit is a Counsellor who will bring us peace and will help us recall the nice things we might have learned about God. However one way he will guide us is by convicting us of sin. Now that does not sound quite so pleasant does it? The Book of Romans says that the Holy Spirit will help us stop sinning and help us to do good things. It also says the Spirit helps us pray and intercedes for us by saying prayers for us, which seems a very nice thing for a busy deity to do.

.

Now this is where Little Kit thinks that he needs to be really clever. He is always a polite little cat and has no desire to upset anyone, least of all God or any element that could be part of any sort of Almighty presence. Remember, in the Bible it suggests that the only sin that cannot be forgiven is blasphemy against the Holy Spirit so it would be a very silly sort of cat who would mess around with that. Little Kit would never intentionally do anything like that due to simple self interest, well we all would. However, you know how peculiar some people can be and what one person uses as simple day-to-day banter another person can take great umbrage and then seek to have them beheaded or maybe even crucified. Humans have always been very odd that way.

As human speech is not his first language Little Kit is always very interested in learning new words and he recently came across a word that was fresh to him and that was the word "Paraclete". He decided to look it up which is exactly what little cats that are unsure about things should do. He has decided to share his findings with you. "Paraclete" means advocate or helper and in respect of Christianity, the term most commonly refers to the Holy Spirit.

For most of you this will be quite a difficult subject to consider, Well you have already discounted the notion that here is a Holy Spirit at all, haven't you. To be honest the whole concept is quite difficult to grasp. At best it must be the result of old men sitting down long ago trying to make sense of all the wonder of the universe. The Holy Spirit sits alongside angels and demons as a fictional device that is used to express some of the more profound issues that mankind has struggled with before becoming enlightened. The Holy Spirit is not logical or scientific and cannot be accurately measured and so the whole notion is utter nonsense and is not worth the bother of any further consideration.

Well, you would not want to be thought of as having a closed mind would you, so just pander to one of Little Kit's odd whims for awhile and see what a black and white cat makes of this particular phenomenon. Most cultures will have some variation on a theme when considering how the universe that we all currently reside in came about.

So we might want to consider what does the Holy Spirit look like? For some reason we all always like to know what things look like even those things that do not actually look like anything. Well even the Bible has a bit of a problem here. At some points it says that the Holy Spirit has the form of a dove, in other places it is like a fire and elsewhere it is like a wind. So that is all a bit confusing.

What is important is the relationship of the Holy Spirit to water. There is the matter of baptism and all that anointment and then believers are made to drink of one spirit. Then there is the claim that it is the Spirit itself that is the living water welling up in Christ. Now that is another of those complex types of descriptions that a simple cat finds hard to completely accept. Then to top all of this there are issues around clouds and shadows and shafts of light. The Holy Spirit as also described as a noise that is "a sound from heaven like the rush of a mighty wind".

For the majority of Christians the "Triune God" is made up of three different people, God the Father, and God the Son and also the Holy Ghost. With each of these three people themselves being God. How complex a deity is that? No wonder all those people are zooming around having nasty old wars with each other.

Little Kit would compare it to a Portuguese man-of-war. This looks like a single sort of jellyfish just bobbing along happily stinging things but that is not what it is at all. It is actually quite a number of different types of animal altogether that have combined to look like a single entity. Perhaps that is not a brilliant description for God, but it works for Little Kit when he tries to explain this to himself. It somehow seems a tad blasphemous and might even be considered as rude, and that would never do.

The New Testament details a close relationship between the Holy Spirit and Jesus himself before his retirement as a human. The lovely Gospels of Luke and Matthew and even the very precise Nicene Creed which hammers it all out says that that Jesus was "conceived by the Holy Spirit and born of the Virgin Mary". The Holy Spirit descended on Jesus like a dove during his baptism and it is noted in his goodbye speak after the final supper they all had together that Jesus promised to send the Holy Spirit to his disciples after his departure. Being a man of his word it says in the tales called the Acts of the Apostles that the arrival of the Holy Spirit happens fifty days after the resurrection of the Christ. This is currently celebrated across the Christian world with the jolly feast they call Pentecost.

In the Acts of the Apostles the reader is reminded that the supernatural elements of the work of Jesus was assisted by the Holy Spirit. He was good at helping to heal sick people and casting out demons but not really practical in helping create a door jamb or fixing wooden scaffolding. Yet it was not all brilliant news; for example in the story noted in Matthews lovely book that it was the Holy Spirit that led Jesus to the desert to be tempted. That is not to say that it did not end well, but on the face of it this does not seem like the nicest thing to do is it?

So there are all kinds of different examples given of the power that is possessed by the Holy Spirit. We can see it was by this power that Jesus was conceived in Mary's holy womb as her virginity was fully maintained. This makes him his Dad. At Jesus was eventually baptised for no good reason by his alleged cousin John the Holy Spirit turned up and flew over Jesus in the form of a dove,

The Holy Spirit is credited with inspiring believers and allowing for them to interpret all the sacred scripture and understand the incantations of all the prophets in both the Testaments. The seven gifts of the Spirit are a very pleasant collection: there is piety, understanding, wisdom, wise council, fortitude, knowledge and a fear of God. Little Kit would suggest that there seems to be a little bit of repetition going on here plus he had a well known preference for kippers, but not in any way that could be construed as blasphemous.

So what does all this religious stuff tell us? Well we can see that this Holy Spirit is very important sort of thing who seems to be responsible for just about everything. Imagine being the person who has the head of John the Baptist which gives you direct access to this power. It is not a belief that would hold much traction in this modern world of rationalism but in Palestine two thousand years ago this was exactly the sort of thing that most people believed was possible. That old gopher wood box was considered as important a thing as ever existed.

38. Consider Properties of Water

Properties of water fact: Water is sticky and if all were normal should really be a gas at room temperature rather than a liquid, but the adhesive properties of its molecules make them uniquely different. This stickiness keeps you alive as water acts to pull blood up narrow vessels in the body, often against the force of gravity.

Like most people who are born on an island Little Kit has a strong affinity and respect for all matters relating to water. He was always keen to highlight its importance in matters to do with baptism, the "Elixir of Life" and many other aspects of religion and the alchemist's art.

At the very simplest level we all know that at room temperature water is an odourless, tasteless, and colourless liquid. It is the most abundant substance on this Earth and and the only common substance to exist in three forms; as a liquid and as a solid and also as a gas on the surface of our planet. Perhaps there are some parallels to be drawn here?

From the way people talk you might think that water only exists on Earth but in fact it is the second most common molecule in the entire known and unknown universe. Not long ago scientists discovered a cloud of vapour surrounding a black hole over twelve billion light years away that has over one hundred and forty trillion times as much water as all that held in the oceans of our world. In fact scientists claim that all the water on Earth arrived in comets and asteroids during the "Late Heavy Bombardment" period about four billion years ago. It is because of pronouncements like these that Little Kit is always sceptical of scientists. If it is true then it must have been quite a difficult exercise to carry out don't you think?

Water is unique because it expands when it freezes, this simple property helps make sure that life on Earth is maintained. No doubt scientists are all very clever but no-one knows why hot water freezes faster than cold water. This is known as the "Mpemba Effect" but even clever sticks Mpemba cannot explain it.

Less than a single percent of the water on Earth is considered as fresh, with ninety-seven percent being salty and the remaining two percent locked up in the polar caps. However life exists on Earth everywhere that there is water even at its most extreme temperatures. No wonder it is such a key component to the elusive "Elixir of Life" that has been sought by so many wise men.

Given that you actually mostly consist of water at about seventy percent and that you have only ten percent of human cells perhaps it would be good if you knew more about it! For instance did you know that the level of water within you changes at various points in your life? When you were a foetus you comprised of ninety-five percent water and this reduced to seventy-seven percent by the time that you were born. You consist of more water in winter than you do in summer.

Brilliant "renaissance men" like Leonardo da Vinci and Niccolo Machiavelli were obsessed with finding out more about water. Of course Little Kit had good reason to really hate water. He had come to realise that water was actually a tool of the Devil and had been invented simple to cause blight on his life. He had always known this. He had realised it when he was an elemental spirit and been forced to travel away from his home when the flood came and drowned the universe. It was water that had divided the continents as they were forced apart in the malice of those days. He had seen the water killing the giants, when they were sucked dry and reduced to bone and dust. He had know that water had been responsible for blinding him when he has been such a happy boy living on Socotra and had been the agent for causing his family to become outcast and despised.

It was water that was the chosen weapon of John the Baptist as he cursed all of humanity by causing the Holy Spirit to enter the souls of the ungodly and allow them to multiply and spread their hate and lies across the face of the globe. It was water that carried the pirates and bolstered their treachery and division and cruelty. It was good old water that had been responsible for the continuation of everything.

It was water that was the chosen weapon of God when he decided that he wanted to wipe out all of mankind in the great flood. He could just of easily have chosen gas or fire or any other method of the many options available to him. It was water that kept Moses afloat when the ancient ones had wanted him drowned. It was water that allowed him to escape from Egypt.

Little Kit had lots of opinions about the hidden meanings of water across both Testaments of the Bible. He just assumed that there were a range of hidden meanings behind the stories of Jesus changing water into wine or walking on the water. Similarly the invention of Moses in the bulrushes and the staff hitting the rock to draw out water all can be seen as highest significant in the secret texts used by ancient alchemists. This is true of so many issues, Lots wife being turned into a pillar of salt is an obvious reference to the chemical changes at the heart of the golden science.

Water is an excellent conductor and helps all kinds of different things to move around. Just think on Earth alone there is waxing and waning, there are waves and erosion; there are tides and all kinds of vibrations and power lines. A while ago, just before he started to be possessed by the spirit of a small cat, Little Kit has read a book that said mankind had been invented by water as a means of transporting itself from one place to another. This had resonated with him and it seems quite true that water is actually very clever indeed. Of course it is a mystery, but all the clues are there and you just need to dig deeper to find out what you really need to know.

39. Consider Puzzling

Puzzling Fact: All living beings need to have a capacity to solve problems. We are all aware that flora and fauna will need to react to any changing circumstances they experience. The same is true for all micro forms from single cells to the most complex life forms.

Have you ever heard of an organisation called Cicada 3301? Now this is quite an interesting modern development and Little Kit was quite drawn to discovering more about it before the time he became possessed and such matters demanding logic became too challenging for him. It has been suggested that this group post puzzles on the internet in order to recruit code breakers from the wider ranks of the general public. They first put a puzzle on the internet on 4th January 2012 and activity has been recorded nearly each year since on that specific date.

It is said that their puzzles are associated with aspects of data security. It has been speculated that the puzzles are a recruitment tool for various security forces or part of a cyber mercenary group. Some have suggested that Cicada 3301 is part of an unknown religious cult. Others have claimed that the Cicada 3301 puzzles are a technological equivalent to the enlightenment journey enjoyed by Western esotericism. Perhaps it is some kind of modern pilgrimage? Little Kit thought that he would have been a very good member of Cicada 3301 had he not contracted vascular dementia, but as things stand he knows that his mental ability is subject to limitations, so might have to wait until his next turn comes around, whatever that might be,

Little Kit had come across numerous secret organisations in his attempt to follow the "Path of Melancholia" arising from the relic box with the shrunken head. Most of the alchemists had to belong to secret societies, The prevailing belief systems of the time were always very suspicious of things that were not included in religious norms whilst still happy to believe in miracles and resurrections. A fear of demons was quite a strong force for much longer than the household use of controlled electricity has been known.

Humans are seen to be born simply to be subjected to the will of nature and then it is inevitable that they will die. The very cleverest of humans were not entirely happy about this prospect and set about finding an alternative. That is the starting point where alchemy comes from.

It is evident that it was the main purpose for the tireless endeavours and scrambling of alchemists throughout the ancient world has been to find the secret to obtaining immortality. The search for the "Philosopher's Stone" to overcome mortality has dominated the wisest of human consciousness since humankind became fully aware of his or her own eventual demise. The inevitability of death and speculation upon the nature of afterlife has always been an object of obsession for mystics and philosophers.

Little Kit was always interested in trying to find out how ideas progress across time and cultures. In particular he was fascinated by the way those stories have been developed in order to explain the deeper mysteries of life. He just adored all the ancient myths that have developed around the world. There is no place anywhere on the planet that does not have some spellbinding explanation for creation and the purpose of existence. These tales are full of colour and describe the rise and fall of Gods and heroes and strange deeds and mystical events. They have morals and ambiguity. Most of the Gods they speak of are immortal so it is perhaps inevitable that humankind would seek to be free from death and pain and to enjoy the same life that is experienced by those who came before.

Even the earliest of recorded tales such as the Epic of Gilgamesh recounts the desire for immortality. Surely you must be interested to know where the ideas behind all these great stories came from. It really is an area of great wonderment and Little Kit is always surprised that humans spend more time working for bits of metal and scraps of paper when they could be doing something that is really very interesting indeed.

You know that many alchemists would spend hours and hours trying to find the elusive "Philosophers Stone" by mixing various metals and minerals at certain times with varying incantations. The basic idea being that they could discover a liquid metal that could be ingested to create longevity and even everlasting pain-free life. Since metals are strong and seemingly permanent and indestructible, it was only rational that whoever ate metal would become equally permanent and indestructible. Due to its fluid nature at room temperature the most obvious contender would have to be mercury or quicksilver as it was known in the past. Unfortunately mercury is very toxic and so many aspiring alchemists would die or encounter madness as a result of trying to drink it. In mythology Mercury is the Roman equivalent for the Greek God Hermes and the Egyptian God Thoth. Little Kit had known many alchemists who had tried to create a solution of gold mixed with quicksilver and none of them had lasted to any great age. Another popular substance they had used was arsenic, which we now know was never going to be a good idea.

Efforts to discover the "Philosopher's Stone" were eventually given pompous titles such as the Magnum Opus, or Great Work. The attempt to turn basic metals like lead into precious metals like gold and silver was a mighty lure. Even more importantly the "Philosopher's Stone" is used to synthesize the "Elixir of Life". It grants unending life, freedom from pain and symbolises perfection, enlightenment, and bliss. The four elements that are Earth, Air, Fire, and Water were seen to have derived from the first ever matter that came out of the original chaos. This original substance was believed to be the key to the "Philosopher's Stone" and alchemists sought to replicate it through a delicate balance of ingredients representing the four cardinal elements.

In this story Little Kit has largely kept to the ancient traditions of the West as he thought this might help you with the general flow of the tale of the head of John the Baptist as it unfolds. However it really is very difficult for him as he really wants to tell you about some of the wonderful traditions that can be found in other parts of the world. For instance many thousands of enjoyable lifetimes could be spent studying the ancient Vedic texts and traditions. Then there are the thousands of variations that are related to the world of sacred plants. Little Kit could bumble on endlessly about the Mushrooms of Immortality or the legend of the Moon Rabbit.

However, all the alchemists in this story have found the underlying principles to their practices in Egypt and so he will leave the subject there.

40 Consider Perplexity

Perplexity fact: There are many more definitions for what perplexity is in comparison to explanations as to why a definition for perplexity is actually needed. Maybe there is a mathematical equation that could accurately explain this for us?

One fine autumn morning Kit the man got out of bed and went to the bathroom where he saw his reflection in a mirror. Looking back at him with a cool and steady gaze was John the Baptist. Of course, he had changed a lot since his hay day when he was alive and pulling in the crowds by the River Jordon. There were three very clear changes that were immediately noticeable. For a start this face was now bright red. When he was fully corporate before his enforced retirement he had been quite dark skinned, as you would expect from someone who had been born in the Levant. Secondly his entire head had reduced in size quite significantly. He had once had a pronouncedly big head in comparison to others and now it was hardly bigger than the size of an average tennis ball. The third thing that was immediately obvious and quite frankly a tad alarming was the fact that it was entirely dismembered. It was just a head apparently floating in space and not at all like the usual corporate sort of faces attached to bodies that Kit had become accustomed to.

Now this was very perplexing to Kit the man. If this was his head floating there in front of him being reflected back in his direction then where on Earth was his usual head?

There are many things that could perplex us. You know the sort of thing: why are we here? Where do we come from? What are we doing? Why doesn't the damn toaster work?

Now the answer to a lot of important questions is gathering an understanding of the origins of things. Take for example carrots. When Little Kit was just a boy all the carrot's he had ever come across were orange. They did not help him see in the dark that was just a hangover from wartime propaganda that used science to lie to us. Kit would like to warn you at this juncture that this sort of thing happens to you on a daily basis, but you do not need to worry about it until the truth becomes revealed to you at the moment that is intended, so you can happily hang around in blindness until then.

There is no point is upsetting you unnecessarily at this point. The future will be just as it always has been; there is nothing you can do to change it now. Anyway, that was one of those sidetracks he sometimes gets caught in, so let's get back to root vegetables. So there he was happy in his understanding of a world that all carrots were happily orange until he read a book that informed him this has not always been the case. Historians and Scientists and Horticulturalists had all agreed that carrot were originally purple and that they came from Afghanistan.

Kit had never been so shocked. He had actually been to Afghanistan in a time before the Russians went so helpful to help them out and he had not seen a purple carrot at all. Then again, there were lots of things in Afghanistan that he had not seen. One thing he did see was the giant statues of Buddha carved into the rock and he had happily skipped around in the passages looking out over the fields of vegetables and in the evening sang songs with wrinkled men who wore turbans and smiled politely at him, It was a bit of a shame the giant statues hewn into the cliff were blown up some years later. He remembered them with fondness. Anyway, this book said that all the carrots in the entire world were purple until they arrived in Holland and it was the Dutch who turned them orange. So well done Holland, not every country can make such a difference, so you should always take pride in your achievements.

Anyway, all of this got Little Kit into thinking about cabbages. He has always thought that cabbages were green and then he discovered that some cabbages were purple. So which came first? Did green cabbages turn purple or did purple cabbages turn green? Then he remembered that there are lots of people dying of starvation in the world and he realised that they would not really mind what colour a cabbage might be as long as they could have one. Well everything seems to be relative. Perhaps someone should discover a law to cover this sort of thing?

Most humans like to experience a level of perplexity in order to use their problem solving skills and chase after such mentally challenging little sticks. For instance if you tell people that even basic history books can advise you that the first pyramids were built over a thousand years before the last woolly mammoth died. Not that they actually know when the first pyramid was actually built, but they do know that the woolly mammoths were still hanging around until 1650 BC even though there seems no obvious reason why they would choose to do so. Perhaps it was one of those addictions to reproduction and breathing that seems to pop up from time to time>

Humans have a basic need to join the dots. They are not exactly cats, but they do have all the equipment they need to try and become good detectives. Kit along with most of the other living creatures in existence felt it was just a bit of a shame they did not try a bit harder. Do you know how every great detective has a bungling policeman who is helping but somehow always gets it completely wrong? Cats think of humans as a sort of developmental Doctor Watson. All the clues are there yet you just slot all the jig-saw puzzle pieces in the wrong place. Perhaps buffoon is just too strong a word for it; what do you think?

41. Consider Pilgrims

Pilgrim Fact: A pilgrim is a traveller and the word can explain a physical journey or a metaphysical pathway to a more holy place. If you are reading this book then it is very likely that you too are a pilgrim. Congratulations. Little Kit really hopes that you get to end up at a place where you find that you actually want to be.

One good things about being a Pilgrim is how it is they always seem to progress. However, none can deny the universal laws of existence and so you might feel a bit sorry for all the anti-Pilgrims who are forced into moving backwards.

Now in this book we have already looked at a few different pilgrims. The one who has held the label most tightly has been the puritan John Howland. So we actually know quite a lot about this particular chap but you might want to discover a little bit more about him? He started of a sperm in his Quaker father Henry and was fertilised in the natural way by his mother Margaret at a place called Fenstanton in Huntingdonshire in 1592. He became the manservant of John Carver in Leiden in the Netherlands. Now it was a scary old time to hold the beliefs that they had because there were other more powerful people who thought different things and so they left on a ship called the Speedwell which proved to be unseaworthy. So it was that all transferred over to another ship called the Mayflower which was deemed more suitable for the intended purpose of getting to America. It was a bright September morning in 1620 that John Howland set off to continue his strange destiny.

Of course we know that he managed to cling desperately onto a rope that just happened to be flailing from the rear of the ship in the midst of a violent swarm. On arrival in the New World he helped found the new colony. He is recorded as being the thirteenth of the forty-one "principal" men to sign the Mayflower Compact. As an indentured servant and also as a freeman in later years he continued on as personal secretary to John Carver who inevitably became the Governor.

Records indicate that it was a harsh winter and this was followed by some exceptionally hot weather indeed. On a particularly baking hot day in April 1621 John Carver dropped into a coma in his cornfield and died soon after. So it was that his former indentured man servant, John Howland, inherited his entire household. Another pretty big slice of luck for John some people might suggest: indeed many people said exactly that. The more kindly folk around had proposed that he was some kind of relative. Anyway, in general terms they were jolly hard times and Little Kit is sure that everyone did their best. Whatever the circumstances, be they entirely innocent or otherwise, John had become a free man and by 1624 he was considered the head of what was once the Carver household. As a result lucky old John was granted an acre for each member of the household including him and the now widowed Elizabeth Tilley to whom he was happily engaged. In 1626, he was one of eight settlers who agreed to assume the colony's debt to its investors in exchange for a monopoly on fur trade. This proved to be another very smart move indeed.

So it was that John Howland, a man who arrived in America as the mere chattel of anther, outlived all but two of the others who sailed on the Mayflower. He died aged eighty whilst his wife, Elizabeth Tilley, outlived her second husband by fifteen years. Their decedents formed a key element of those considered Harvard's 'intellectual aristocracy' and key shapers of the political direction of the United States. All based on the extra wiggle of one little sperm and a stray rope trailing from an old wooden boat tossed around in a storm. Perhaps there were some different factors at play here. Perhaps there is some strange merry dance that we do not yet understand. What do you think?

On the face of it John Howland has nothing what-so-ever to do with the finding of the head of John the Baptist. Why did you think he would? However, Little Kit was tracing a thread of melancholia and whilst the lines of the journey drew quite close across time, he never located an actual clear connection. So it is that the entire universe seems to have near misses or secrets that remain unsolved. Little Kit was glad that John Howland never got hold of the head of John the Baptist, he thinks the world would be a very different place now if that had happened.

42. Consider Power Differentials

Power Fact: In the beginning was the word. It does not take much effort to realise that the concept of the power of words is a universally accepted reality.

Little Kit was not a great fan of the Book of Proverbs in the Bible; he found them all a little bit too preachy for the uncomplicated life a cat chooses to live. There is one particularly pertinent bit that says "The tongue has the power of life and death and those who love it will cat its fruit". Now Kit the man had become a cat and he can no longer speak so has lost this particular power, along with most others As first it was frustrating, but then he got used to the way things had developed. Now he had nothing to say anymore so it is not really an issue of concern to him at all. It's funny how things can change like this.

Of course you fully understand that all words hold some element of power. If all the songs you like just repeated the single word "cheese" over and over again they would not provoke the same emotions in you. So then you might want to think about the differences in power that words might have. You can start off at the basics; is the word "No" more powerful than the word "Yes"? There are a whole range of both obvious and invisible reasons that lie behind the power of words. For example you probably will think that the word "tiger" evokes" a greater sense of danger than the word "maggot" because of the image that it evokes. However, you are much more likely to get eaten by and become a maggot than you are to be eaten by and become a tiger.

Now this is one of those forests that Little Kit can get himself utterly lost in and so he needs to get to the point fairly quickly. You might think that the word "death" is scary. Well, given that it announces the end of life then it does have a level of power. There are words like "Armageddon" or "Annihilation" or "Genocide" that try to explain very powerful sort of ending and hold a certain level of power. Behind all of that there is a simple little word that is far more hurtful and destructive than these, and most people do not actually realise it until it touches their lives. Now the actual word "dementia" sounds fairly innocuous doesn't it? Certainly when Kit the man was first diagnosed he just took it in his stride and thought that he could bravely carry on, just like he would with any other illness. Sadly, it is not quite as simple as that. No matter how brave a person wants to be or how strong they think they might be the battle is already lost. The enemy has an overwhelming power of blackness and pestilence and destruction that you simply cannot comprehend. It is like a maggot trying to fight against a crashing angry mighty ocean. It is not a contest. It is a slow and cruel and inevitable stripping away of everything and it just laughs as a hollow and empty shell remains with futile whimpering and the complete loss of everything. It is just so powerful that no words can come close to describing its compassionless bleakness. Who would have thought that a simple single word like "dementia" would have the power to outstrip all of creation, all of hope, all of being? Yes, it really is a word you want to try and keep away from if you can.

So you are aware that over the years various people have said spells to try and make things happen. It is not something that is particularly made obvious in modern life, but if you think about it for a moment you will see that people respond to the things that you say in the way that you expect them to. So there is a simple power in that. All ancient communities have their preferred spells and words of wisdom. The importance of naming something cannot be over emphasised, which is why it is import to name children wisely. Can you imagine what life would be like for someone called Blancmange going through our school system? It would inevitably cause a few issues that a liberal modern thinking parent might wish to avoid.

We now arrive at the word "procession". The ownership of something is usually seen as good and to be owned is usually seen as bad. When John Howland was not a free man but an indentured servant those who did not own him might have considered his position as being less favourable when a few years later he was established as a free man, Little Kit did not really want to possess the soul of Kit the man in any negative way, he just wanted to make use of a soul that was lying there vacant. Little Kit the cat could justify the reality of his possession of the soul of demented old Kit the man by telling himself that he was actually helping his host. It was not abuse it was a partnership of convenience, even though just one of the parties involved understood what was happening.

There are nowadays words that are so taboo that no-one can say them and remain unscathed. Perhaps it has always been that way?

43. Consider Pheromones

Pheromone Fact: A pheromone is a small chemical that triggers a social response. So can you think of how many hormones may have had an impact on you during the time you have spent up until now reading this tale?

Now quite a lot of this story has been about consequences and how little things can have an impact on big things. Now because Little Kit the cat is a detective he is always eager to clearly see the trail that the clues uncovered have lead back to. Remember he had lived very, very many lives and so had lost his virginity on almost an equal number of occasions. Let's face it. He was a victim of the same universal forces that plague us all and so had as good a grasp on such matters as anyone else. One of the things that evoke primeval urges and causes all sorts of serious consequences are pheromones. You will probably have never seen one because they are pretty tiny but you and everyone and everything else is here because of them. Little Kit is pretty sure that most people do not spend too much of their daily lives thinking about the relationship they have to this particular aspect of their being. Existence is a cruel invention sometimes.

So what are the shared qualities of myrrh and frankincense that are important to this story? What was the force that caused Herod to be quite so generous in response to a dance? In essence, Kit tried to find a reason to understand why people end up doing the strange things they do. You know that you will have done strange things and thought particular thoughts and acted in ways that you did not think you normally might and there are lots and lots of reasons behind this. Most of them humans do not even know about yet, because the road you are taking is still very much the start of a journey. Whether or not it is a long journey is subject to endless variables; the universe is full of diverse opportunities and significant pitfalls. Maybe you will end up trapped in the sticky amber of the age waiting endlessly to re-emerge into the sunlight? Everything is possible but some things are more probable than others.

The word "pheromone" was only created in 1959 Of course, as you will have guessed, they happily existed before that but no-one had a name for them. Now they are devious little blighters that have caused all sorts of problems since they first came into being. They are actually quite interesting if you can get the time to consider them. One key point is that most sex pheromones are produced by the females; only a small percentage of sex attractants are produced by males. Who would have thought? Pheromones also exist in plants which can be jolly helpful to them, for example when being grazed upon some species will produce alarm pheromones resulting in increased tannin production in neighbouring plants which make them less appetizing to any hungry herbivore that is coming to eat them all up.

Little Kit is always keen to try and explain more about this connectivity where plants clearly exchange information with others, just as all of nature is able to do. Kit does not understand how mankind is quite so blind to the shimmering and obvious fact that the only reasonable explanation is that it us a fundamental process of "The Great Lie" Your eyes have been poked out and you do not know it! Some female insects use pheromones to warn other female insects to stay away from the area where they have laid their eggs. Pheromones come in different strengths and varieties. Your scientists discovered that they can cause attraction for butterflies from a distance of over six miles. Of course your scientists have still got rather a lot to learn!

Kit would place money in betting that you have never thought too much about how pheromones have affected you. You are aware that you have reacted in ways that you did not think you would in certain situations, but did you really believe that you were being totally manipulated by some invisible little things that you did not know were there. You are a human so you are in charge; no invisible nothingness is going to boss you around! That sort of thing only happens to other people doesn't it!

Cabbage white caterpillars lay down pheromone tracks to show following munching chums the way forward. How do you think that your family got to where they are now?

So now you have discovered that even though you thought that you were fully one hundred percent human at the start of this book you are, in fact, only ten percent human. At the start of this tale you thought that you were largely in control of what you do and that you have an understanding of why you might do it. Now you have come to a point where you should realise that you have very little actual say in what you do. You are just an animal subject to the various invisible and unknown forces that drive us to and fro in this carousel of absurdity. There is magnetism and gravity there are hormones and wishes. You are the magic because the magic is in you and around you. You are time and you are death. You are life ad you are pestilence. You are the stalk and leaves of the cabbage where the vital juices flow and the space between the leaves where other lives may prosper.

44, Consider Power by Politics

Power by Politics fact: Even Moses understood that the control of laws is the key to power. He ended up taking two tablets to try and make it all better.

It was not until Little Kit took an astral journey to the Sultanate of Fez in the late sixteenth century that he unlocked the clue that told him why it was that he had found the head of John the Baptist in s shed in Cardiff some four hundred and fifty years later. It was so blindingly obvious that he could not believe he had not realised the truth of the situation earlier. Still, it is always easy to be wiser after any event isn't it?

The more observant of you might have noticed that the "Pathway of Melancholia" Little Kit had been following has been very closely entwined with the bloodline of the Mendoza's. Now the first actual contact they had with the gopher box was the moment that it was removed from the treasury of the Sultan of Fez by Samuel Pallache. The earliest that Little Kit could firmly establish any Mendoza was a series of Rabbi's who lived in the region of Fez in Morocco and other Jewish enclaves across this region Northern Africa a few hundred years earlier. He could not tell if the family had any proven dealings with the powerful sultans but it did not seem a mere coincidence that these two investigative pathways should have crossed. It was also evident from research that the Mendoza family had strong links to the far more ancient bloodlines descending from the fold of Aaron.

Without needing to go into too much detail you need to understand a little bit about the complex political events that were impacting on the region before the box was taken away from Fez. There were a few key Berber families who were particularly powerful and had a great sway over Morocco. The two families that are important in this particular tale are the Wattasid dynasty and the Marinid dynasty. As you would have guessed the two families were related and the Marinids were originally in the ascendency and recruited many of their viziers from from the

Wattasids. History books will tell you that these then assumed the role of the more powerful Sultans eventually seizing control when the last Marinid was murdered during a popular revolt in Fez in 1465. Well. to be fair, he had been responsible for the massacre of many of the Wattasids six years earlier and so in the greater scheme of things that might be seen as being quite a just and reasonable sort of result. The first Sultan of the Wattasid dynasty controlled the northern part of Morocco whilst the south was divided into several principalities.

So was the Wattasid dynasty a good thing? Well it was clear that in general terms Morocco was seen as being in a state of decline when they come into power. The rulers of the Marinid dynasty had faced some hostilities from various Portuguese and Spanish invasions. Meanwhile the Wattasids accumulated absolute power through political manoeuvring. Well the Marinids got very grumpy indeed when they discovered the extent of the conspiracy against them so they slaughtered the Wattasids, leaving only one chap alive. Yet this was a mistake as he proved to be a cunning sort of fellow and it was he who founded the Kingdom of Fez and established th e dynasty to be succeeded by his decedents. He was also one of those fellows who could hold a grudge.

In the world of dynasties it was not a really long lasting sort of affair. Following a battle in an awful place named Tadla the once mighty Wattasids were replaced as rulers by the warrior like princes of the Saadi dynasty who came from an equally awful place called Tagmadert. These princes had ruled all of southern Morocco for forty years and were rather used to all this sort of thing by now.

Now, unlike their predecessors, these Saadi princes were not members of the sacred society that was known as the "Keepers of Aaon's Promise" and knew nothing of its rules or its treasures. They did not even know that they had important relics in their treasury and certainly did not miss them when they were gone. In fact they had a great many other problems to cope with as the entire area was ravaged by discourse and political unrest and general decline. Was this a coincidence? Well, Little Kit would always suggest that there is no such thing as a coincidence.

Following the departure of the box containing the head of John the Baptist Morocco endured a prolonged multifaceted crisis. They declined in every serious political concern including economic, political, social and cultural issues. Population growth remained stagnant and all the previously flourishing towns and cities became increasingly impoverished. Meanwhile the intellectual life which had been so buoyant was very clearly on a very marked decline.

The Wattasid rulers failed in their promise to protect Morocco from foreign incursions. In the south, the fierce war-loving princes of the Saadian dynasty were in the ascendant when they defeated the Portuguese on the coast at Agadir. Their military successes contrast with the Wattasid policy of appeasement and conciliation with the Roman Catholic kings to the north. As a result, the people of Morocco tended to regard the Saadians as heroes, making it easier for them to retake the Portuguese strongholds on the coast. The Saadians also attacked the Wattasids who were forced to yield to the new power. It all came to a sorry sort of end, for when the last Wattasids fled Morocco by ship they were captured and murdered by pirates. This was a good time for pirates and a bad time for Wattasids.

Little Kit had been quite sad to learn of the fate of the Wattasids as he had always enjoyed visiting them and had found them all to be very hospitable and easy to get on with. If only they had been able to keep hold of the box and not allowed it to be stolen by Samuel Pallache who knows how things might have turned out?

45. Consider Proficiency

Proficiency Fact: Your belly button used to be your mouth.

So if you asked Little Kit what might be his favourite butterfly he might well have suggested that it was the "cabbage white"; but of course, that would not have been true? No-one really thinks of the plain old "cabbage white" as their favourite butterfly when there are so many more colourful options to consider. As a very ancient soul indeed Little Kit had pre-existed butterflies by some considerable distance, At the time that they turned up the rest of the universe seemed to favour them very much as they brightened the place up a bit with their strange flitting and all the other effects they brought to the table. As you are acutely aware Kit was always very interested in the arena of "cause and effect". He would sit under the scruffy bush in a happy meditation for simply hours at a time wondering what would have happened if Jesus had been born a girl, or if Eve had decided that she was already too full of figs to really want to eat anything else or if God had decided to call his chosen people Palestinians. He loved all that kind of stuff. Who doesn't?

Now Little Kit has been around for a very long time indeed. He is an ancient soul after all. However, he was far from being the first thing that popped a pretty and inquisitive head out of the vortex of the beginning that constantly occurs. Before him there were angels and before angels there were even more ancient souls. These were generally known as the "First Ones" and they were generally held in pretty high regard. Surprisingly across the eons their paths had never really crossed that much but Little Kit was pretty sure that the soul of Jesus had played host to one of those most special ones who the angels had called the sons of God.

Whatever his lineage, be it transparent or opaque Kit was pretty sure Jesus would have had a very close allegiance to a creator God and the Holy Spirit. Whatever the exact nature of their relationship he was pretty sure it would be far too complex for a small black and white cat of average intelligence to fully understand.

So we are coming the last parts of this particular story. Little Kit was well aware that he had presented the reader with lots of different facts and characters and hoped that they were of interest to those who had stayed loyal. There was one more particular thread that he wanted to expand on and that was the potted history of the Knights of the Order of Calatrava who you may remember were mentioned in respect of the early life of Juan Ponce de Leon. This was just one of those loose ends that he felt you would want him to tie up.

This Order was a military organization that was founded in the south of Castile following a request by monks who felt a compelling need to become warriors as soldiers of the cross. In 1164 Pope Alexander III issued one of his many papal bulls which confirmed the Order of Calatrava as a recognised militia. The main catalyst was a very fervent Abbot with the name of Raymond who was one of those people that eventually became a saint for his efforts. As a peace loving cat Little Kit was always a bit perplexed when men of God got together to kill other humans and then were made saints, but for the purposes of this story he will let that ride for the moment.

Calatrava is the Arabic name of a Castilian castle that was recovered from the Muslims in 1147 by King Alfonso the Seventh. It was agreed by those who decided such matters that it would be useful if the non-ordained ancillary staff the Abbeys could form a band of fighting knights to confront those who followed the path of Islam. It is said that they were originally motivated by the desire for religious rewards and that pecuniary benefits only claimed dominance some time later. This was quite a familiar pattern for those like Kit who follow with interest the history of mankind. When the Abbot Raymond died in 1163 and wandered off into sainthood a chap called Don Garcia started to lead them in battle as their first Grand Master.

In 1187 the Knights of Calatrava gained definitive rule which was approved by the very strange Pope Gregory the Eighth. This rule imposed upon the knights three religious vows: the rules of silence in the refectory, dormitory, and oratory; the rule of abstinence on four days a week and they were also obliged to recite a fixed number of paternosters for each day. Strangely they were also ordered to sleep in their armour: well you can never be too careful can you? Popes could make up all sorts of strange laws and rules in those days and Little Kit found many of them to be quite amusing.

The first military actions of the Knights of Calatrava were highly successful, However the Moorish leaders needed to reassert themselves and so the knights were faced with a new wave of invading Islamic warriors from Morocco and soon after things did not go quite so well. A major encounter resulted in a defeat for Castile at the pivotal Battle of Alarcos. It was a pretty disastrous reverse of fortune for the Christians and the knights were forced to abandon their stronghold of Calatrava to the Moors. The scattered remains of Castilian knights sheltered in the various local monasteries and began to regroup in secret.

To help reverse the loss the pope they decided to call Innocent the Third summoned foreign crusaders to join the Iberian Christians. An early battle in the re-conquest was at Calatrava in1212 which was returned to its former masters. This marked the decline of Muslim power and the climax of Iberian chivalry: In 1212 a chap who loved his titles named King Ferdinand the Saint captured Cordoba which had been the capital of the old caliphate.

Throughout all these skirmishes Kit was convinced that the head of John the Baptist would have been a very great prize, but somehow the various Great

Priests and acolytes who formed the "Keepers of Aaon's Promise" managed to ensure the safety of the Holy relic as various religious groups battled fiercely with each other all around.

At this point the European crusade seemed at an end. However, as Little Kit has frequently pointed out to you humans do not always act in the best interests of the rest of the universe. Encouraged by various victories over the enlightened Moors the Christians decided to seek to press home their advantage. Ferdinand's successor, the inappropriately named Alfonso the Tenth the Wise planned for a crusade in the East and contemplated marching with his Castilian knights to restore the former Latin Kingdom of Jerusalem. What possible harm could that possibly do? Well their God would surely be very pleased! Now there were lots of cities dotted all over the world that were deemed as important. Yet Alfonso X had decided that it was desirable to take all of Europe into a war at the very place where the head of John the Baptist had been parted from his body. Little Kit smelled a rat.

We now come to a grand-master of Calatrava who features on the "Path of Melancholia". He was called Pedro Giron. Using all his skills as a detective Little Kit had discovered that he was part of the Mendoza bloodline and very closely connected to the awful conquistador whose name he could never remember. Kit had found that Giron belonged to an eminent Castilian family descending from Portugal. History has painted him as an ambitious intriguer who was more anxious about his family interests than about those of his order. When Little Kit has visited him on his astral travels he has always found Pedro to be both charming and amusing.

Giron offered assistance to King Henry IV in his various wars and squabbles and in return was offered the hand of Henry's sister, the remarkable Isabella the First of Castile. Pedro Giron had already had his personal vow of celibacy annulled the amenable Pope Pius the Second, who also granted to Pedro the great privilege of resigning his high dignity in favour of his illegitimate son, Rodrigo Telles Giron, a child eight years old. In effect this meant that the leadership of the order was passed over to a committee of advisors. It was an interesting time of great political intrigue and manipulation. Events took a strange turn in 1466 when Pedro suddenly died when on his way to the court to get wed. Observers have suggested that this saved the future Queen of Castile from an unworthy consort. Perhaps it was just a coincidence?

It was the fall of Granada in 1492 that led to the gradual decline of the Order. They had been established to overcome the Moors and mow the Muslims had been defeated. The purpose of the Order had been achieved and they were now superfluous to requirements. However, they did not jut immediately disband and disappear. They were still around nearly fifty years later when Pope Paul the Third who was not at all as innocent as his predecessors commuted their vow of celibacy to one of conjugal fidelity. They were still there in 1652 when under the mighty Philip the Fourth they took a new vow: that of defending the doctrine of the "Immaculate Conception". This was the last major manifestation of any religious spirit in the orders. The military spirit, too, had long since disappeared. The last attempt to employ the knights for a military purpose was that of Philip IV, in quelling the rebellion of the Catalans in 1640, So it can be seen that most of the political and military power of the Order dissipated by the end of the 15th century yet the final dissolution of the order's property did not occur until 1838. Extinction can be a long old process!

So what has this short history lesson got to tell us about the journey of the old box that had the bright red shrunken head of John the Baptist inside? Well you need to remember that maxim that Little Kit uses and dig a little deeper.

We know that the box was being kept in Cordoba and the city prospered. We can see that when Fatima of Madrid moved the box away that the city declined. It then went on a journey. It went to Fez, and the city prospered, when it left the city declined. It briefly went to the Caribbean which suddenly became a centre for prosperity. It then passed through Plymouth which turned from a dull backwater to a place where things briefly started to happen. It then went to Amsterdam and that became a centre of great import. The box then came back with the Mendoza family to London which thrived as being a centre for commerce and the arts ever since. Now it has arrived in Cardiff. Keep an eye out for big things to start happening in South Wales. Remember, there is no such thing as coincidence.

46. Consider Party-time

Party-time Fact: On 28th June 2009 Professor Stephen Hawking held a party for time travellers, but no-one turned up.

You may have noticed that this story has rather skipped over the events of two important parties. The first happened on Socotra when the baby Pharouk was born into the world. His Mum and Grandmother carried him back from the caves of Haq to where the remainder of the family were tending their goats and bees. Any birth on the island was a joyous occasion and this was better than most because a prophecy had been delivered. It was clear that this tiny newcomer was going to rise to prominence. What was not to celebrate?

Another major event we noted was the birthday of Herod when the dancing girl caused him to make a very rash promise. This one event spawned the ledged of the dance of the seven veils. That is just artistic nonsense; there were no veils, just the same old seedy process that has happened in all civilisations before and since where older men get involved with sexual ogling of much younger women. Such practices in humans have always tended to follow that pattern rather than the other way around. Pheromones may be tiny but they are potentially lethal; they are also a poor excuse for seediness.

Little Kit had found the recorded guest list for the birthday party of King Herod Antipas to be quite revealing. There have been a few examples in this tale where the political machinations of various tyrants have come into become inextricably linked to the progress of the head. If you threw a birthday party and had invited all of the top ranking officials and army officers and leading citizens of the region that might say something about you. If you happened to arrange for someone to be beheaded and a head brought on a plate into the assembled gathering it would say even more about you. As it happens in his astral travels Little Kit had never been very fond of Herod, he found him to be something of a bully.

It might seem a bit odd given what we know now but Little Kit had always quite liked Queen Herodias. He felt she had been exploited quite savagely by Philip the Tetrarch and then after she had been forced to divorce him ended up being forced to marry his more horrid brother Herod. Of course he did not like her role in the beheading but was able to understand that she was in an impossible position and the path she followed was virtually preordained for her. There are many similar examples of this across history that Little Kit could expand on, but that would be another of those issues that would deflect us from the narrative of this particular story. Surely we have had enough of those!

Now you know how at the end of any great detective novel the investigator invites all of those suspected of the crime to gather together so that the clues can be discussed and the truth revealed. Kit had considered having a similar arrangement and inviting all of the key characters from the entangled "Pathway of Melancholia" to join together in his lounge and share what he had found.

He started to think of who he would need to invite. Well it would start with Pharouk and possibly his mother and grandmother as it would be nice for them to all meet up again and to discuss all that had happened to them since. Then he thought that he would need to invite the body of John the Baptist as he might like to be able to meet up with his head again. It would be nice to have John's Mother and Father come along too as they had always been considered as being nice people. Of course Jesus would always be welcome, if anyone knew how to behave at a supper party it was him. Kit decided that he would not want to invite any of the twelve disciples as they would probably want to boast of all their different achievements and might overshadow the passage of the gopher box, which would be the main focus of this planned event.

He would then need to invite Philip the Alchemist and Zosimos as they had played such an important part in preserving John's head so well. He would need to invite Maslama al-Majriti and his daughter Fatima and it would be another family reunion that would almost certainly be joyous.

Little Kit had to think quite carefully about who we would invite next. Obviously Samuel Pallache would need to be there, but he was not sure if the nameless conquistador and even Juan Ponce de Leon should be added. He would need to think about that. Then he came onto the Mendoza's. There was the old butcher and Daniel and the Frederick and Amelia Aarons. Her husband Little Douggie Hiscox would need to join the party and of course their son David who was the man that Kit the cat processed and who actually owned the small terraced house that would host the event. Then he thought that he might need to invite the Holy Spirit. Well it would be only polite, but how on Earth would he set a place at the table for him?

Well the invitation list was just one thing; then Kit started to think about what food he would need to serve. Well there were Gnostics and Jews and Muslims and Christians, perhaps the only reasonable choice would be some sort of fish offering? What about those who were vegans? That was another headache.

Of course there would not be an awful lot of room. The two bedded terraced house in Cardiff had just a twenty foot long lounge that was about ten foot wide. That would be quite a crush. Now what sort of music might they all enjoy? It would have to be something with a Middle Eastern heart, but there were a lot of generations to try and encompass and human fashions can change quite significantly over time. Certainly folk music does not seem as popular as once it did. Maybe something with a lute would be the suitable option?

Little Kit wondered if there should be some kind of entertainment or party games, He could not see twister of sardines being particularly popular. Charades was always a winner but all of the potential guests had such a wide range of cultural references that any such activity would almost certainly prove to be frustrating for someone, perhaps even all of them!

The more that he thought about it the more problems he envisaged in his mind and so, in the end, Little Kit abandoned the idea altogether and resigned himself to the fact that no such gathering of the key figures included in this story would take place at all.

A gathering was out of the question and Kit had decided that he needs to consider something else now to try and draw all the strands of his journey together. The land of Palestine and all its surrounds were a very active sort of place two thousand years ago. There was all the activity that surrounds the arrival and departure of angels from their various levels of heaven and thousands of Roman soldiers and officials rushing around conquering sandy places. It was a location that Little Kit had visited quite a lot in his astral travels and investigations because there are always lots of clues laying around in the various writings that survive. Of course, it was a time before alchemy was officially recognised but its practices still took place all over the region and beyond. You will appreciate that there were many secret organisations to help hide whatever it was that the alchemists did not want to be disclosed.

So it was that Philip the Alchemist belonged to just such an organisation that steeped themselves in arcane mysteries, secret handshakes, ugly aprons and power struggles. Before the mantle was granted onward to Pharouk Philip had become the Great Priest of the "Keepers of Aaon's Promise" at an important time. To those who followed more conservative belief systems they were considered quite a dodgy bunch even then, They had built up quite a reputation because they employed various assassins and had acquired a great deal of wealth. Little Kit was able to ascertain that the gopher box with the head of John the Baptist was originally stored in the palace of Herod not far from Jerusalem,

However, it was not there for very long and it followed an unusual path up to Caeserea Philippi and then Lebanon before heading southwards into Egypt. It stayed hidden away for many years as it was felt that the power it held was too great for any of the masters to properly control. This was the state of affairs until Zosimos of Panopolis became a leader of a Gnostic group that was one of the many offshoots of the "Keeper of Aaon's Promise". At this point the increasingly reddening head of John the Baptist was kept in a guarded underground chamber that was being used as a treasury for all of the important items that had been gathered. The box, along with all the other relics and artefacts were being carefully guarded well away from all the hustle and bustle of the more powerful tyrants and thieves of the day.

We have seen how the box was moved across various strongholds of the "Keepers of Aaon's Promise" across Northern Africa and Southern Europe before being located in Cordoba. Then it was moved by Fatima to Fez where it was later taken by Samuel Pallache. It then took a brief journey to the Caribbean and so the Plymouth, Amsterdam and London before ending up being found in Cardiff. It was clear to Little Kit that this was not a journey that had happened by accident. So he had felt that he needed to dig deeper. That is just the way that the mind of a small black and white cat with a penchant for detecting seems to work!

Kit actually knew all of the towns and cities the head of John the Baptist had been taken too on his travels really well as he had lived in every single one of them in his various astral journeys and the sharing of souls with different locals. Of course they were all on the routes taken by various refugee groups leaving troubled lands to seek peace. These are the same towns and cities that refugees from places like Somalia and Syria visit in modern times. Perhaps it had something to do with that? Which of us really knows the secret machinations of the ancient powers?

47. Consider Power by Osmosis

Power by osmosis fact: The word "osmosis" was not coined until the 1700s but as an engineering principle it was used in the building of the great pyramid at Giza. Just because something does not yet have a name does not mean it is not there!

We come to the conclusion of this nice little story. Kit was now all curled up cosily on his bed while considering the best way to sum up everything so any reader could feel there was a satisfactory conclusion to the shared journey they had invested so much effort into. Let's face it; Kit was nothing if not decent in that way.

He had already completed his first walk around the garden for the day. The little brown and white cat had left messages in all the usual places, mainly over by the shed and also around the tree planted over the forgotten graves of the two martyrs that had been hung in a previous time. He did not have much time for the other cats as he had lived long enough to know what they were really all about. As you many know the brown and white cat was a bit less offensive to him that most of them. He could smell the traces that the black cat that was being possessed by the horrid ancient spirit Pugnance had walked along the small wall earlier in the day, just spying in him as usual. This happened most days and so he had developed a good coping strategy to deal with this so that it did not cause him too much anxiety and distress nowadays.

So he was mostly calm and free to consider the key aspects of this particular journey. As always, the most important thing to remember in every case he was involved in was the underlying principle of, what the ancient souls and the "First Ones" would call "The Great Lie".

It has been established that you are almost certainly going to be a minimum of ten percent human if you are reading this. You will certainly be old enough to realise that everything that you know, everything you have been told and everything you have ever experienced or thought is completely and utterly untrue. So it is a hard thing for you to understand and will have caused you some conflict in the past because you are not entirely stupid.

You know there are millions of people in the world who are starving whilst there are many others who spend their time wandering what is the best wallpaper to buy to go with their furniture or what is the best way to cook and serve monkfish. Yes the world is not fair, everyone knows it and no one is remotely interested in changing that. You know that humans are in a state of constant warfare and these things do not happen by accident. Maybe you think there are too many foreigners in your country? That seems to be a pretty common and utterly irrational viewpoint nowadays. Maybe you think that your country is better than some other country? Maybe you like the Eurovision song contest? Oh, there are just so very, very many false paths these types of considerations Kit could go down, but he knows that he needs to be a bit disciplined here otherwise everything will end up a bit too mushy.

So let's think about religion for a moment because that is a point of reference that Kit often comes to. It is not that he is remotely a cat of any belief himself, because he was there at the start and will be that at the end which will never happen and has already happened. However there are lots of people all over the place dotted all through the time that is both reality and also has never happened who firmly believe all sorts of things. Let's start at the beginning, even though there was no beginning. God created the world in seven days. For most of the time people actually believed that this was literally seven days and now many people actually believe that the seven days was not actually seven days at all. Some people actually think there is a God; others actually think that there cannot be a God. Some people think this God who may or may not actually be is kind and loving and omnipresent, others firmly believe that God is cruel and unjust and some sort of intergalactic baddie. So what do you think?

Anyway, you will have worked out that if cabbages have only been around for a thousand years or so then it is pretty unlikely that Jesus ever even ate one. He was probably more used to artichokes. Anyway, what else did he eat? Well it is pretty obvious by now that he actually ate the gold and frankincense and myrrh that he was given by the travelling alchemists. They had discovered that these are key components to the procedure that will produce the "Elixir of Life". This is how he was able to raise Lazarus, this is how he was able to heal the sick, this is why he was able to raise from the grave. You do not have to be much of a detective to realise that all the clues are there. All you really need to do is consider the actuality of the dispersal of power by the process of osmosis. There is no need to dig any deeper as it is a clear as clear can possibly be.

Of course Jesus was surprised when a caravan turned up where he was camping and invited him to go over to assist Philip the Alchemist in his perpetrations. He knew that the Holy Spirit was still present in the head of John the Baptist; it was his cousin after all! He knew more than any other person of the power that the relic of the prophet contained. Jesus was always very proud of his carpentry work, but there were lots of other joiners that Philip could have chosen, so he fully understood that he was being requested for reasons other than his skills in making boxes and shaping wood.

Many people have speculated on what Jesus did after he went to the Temple of Jerusalem and impressed them with his knowledge of the scriptures in his early teens and then turning up age the age of thirty to start his ministry. There are lots of rumours and stories that he went to India or travelled around Arabia and very few mention Egypt even though the Bible clearly states that he went there. Not many people have speculated that he became a major alchemist and had a clear understanding of the Holy practices. It is almost as if there has been a conspiracy of silence. You will be aware that it has been suggested that there has been similar conspiracies in respect of his possible bloodline, or the true nature of his relationship to the much maligned Mary. Gossip is nothing new!

Remember Kit is keen that you take notice of the "Great Lie". It should be very obvious to you by now that everything you have ever been told about everything is utterly and completely untrue. If you were lonely bacteria in the animal of some animal you would still be affected by black holes, even if you did not understand what they are and their implications to you. You would be swishing around in some moderately happy warm ignorance wouldn't you? No doubt you think that they are simple little things that have no understanding of philosophy or of history or hold any interest at all in what they have been and where they are going. So you need to think a little bit more about the connectivity that binds us all, for they are you and you are them. You are the stomach, you are the black holes and you are the space in between. You are living in the fields that lie beyond good deeds and bad thoughts. You are a part of the beginning and are equally a part of the end, just as everyone else that has ever been has been and will be. You are mighty and you are small. You are a pirate, you are a boxer, you are a trader and you are a prophet. You are water and you are mineral and vegetable and animal. You are thought and movement just as you are silence and warmth and frost. You are the stone and you are the wind. You are the soil and you are the sky. You are a sinner and you are holy. All of the universe resides within you and can contentedly reside without you. You are blindness and you are sight. You are the mystery and you are the discovery. You are the question as you are the answer.

Well as you can work it out because you have a developed brain that allows you to weigh up all the evidence, it really does not matter what you think. Do you really think that God or the world is going to exist or change or care just because something invisible has happened in your mind to make you think whatever it is that you have thought? But then we have the matter of the bacteria, just one tiny little unseen wiggle and the entire world is changed. At one time half of you was a just a tiny sperm zooming along. You looked identical to all the thousands of brothers and sisters you had and were essentially exactly the same, but then here you are now and where are they? You probably only exist because you did one tiny invisible little wiggle more than your brother or sister who you left behind to die in a strange mucus soup. How could you? Well we all did, so get over it. Unless, of course, that was not how it happened at all and you have a better explanation!

So then we can think about the various religious figures that people have chosen to follow, because strangely enough these are actually the best way for a messenger like Little Kit to tell you the truth about the "Great Lie". Of course, you already know the essence of the matter in your soul. Perhaps you are of the view that you innately know what is right and what is wrong. The question of the origins of morality is just as interesting as the consideration given to the origins of anything, whether they exist or do not exist

So let us stat with Adam and Eve. Do you believe that the human race started with two people happily created in a nice little garden over by the Euphrates River? Perhaps you prefer a more scientific approach that we all come from a small family who developed somehow in the Rift Valley in Ethiopia. Perhaps you are a little bit more left wing and feel that we were created by aliens to dig gold for them. Perhaps you follow the evolutionist's viewpoint and that we slowly built our way up from fishes and apes to become whatever we are now. There might be those who do not think that we actually exist at all and that we are all just part of the deranged imaginings of something bigger and wiser and older altogether. There are lots of creation stories from all over the world that throw some light into the dark pit of how we actually got here, or ever if we got here at all. Perhaps there is not even a here for us to be in? It is all quite a lot for a small black and white cat to be considering on his day off.

Then there was Jesus. Or was there? Anyway there are millions and millions of people who like to think that Jesus was a mighty prophet. Some say he was the son of God and then that makes him a third of a God and that he overcame death and died on the cross to carry the sins of man and that he was altogether a very good thing. Then there are lots of people who think well some of that is true but there are bits about it that do not really feel comfortable and develop a belief system that works nicely for them. Of course the majority of people in the world are not from a Christian background and so have been brought up to believe other truths and Jesus is not even a consideration or known of. So you have to ask the question which of all the religious belief systems of the world is actually true. Of course the answer is that they are all true. Conversely, they cannot all be true can they? So some of them, inevitably, must be untrue. So which religion is untrue? The answer, of course, is that they all are. Oh dear, it is all a bit of a muddle isn't it?

So then we come to science. We all know that science relies entirely on things that can be proven. You simply cannot argue with hard facts and actual physical evidence; or perhaps you can? Surely most of science must be true otherwise all our toasters would not work and we would have to darken our bread by other means. Sadly Little Kit has some bad news for you. All the truth that you believe in science is actually a lie. It is a great shame as he really quote likes the concept of science as being the harbinger of truth, but his experience has shown him at is simply fails to deliver. However, almost all of the ancient souls would say that it is a really good try. Well done, keep pressing on.

So what do the angels think of it all. Well everyone knows there are no such things as angels. To even bring them into the discussion is madness. Yet, you may have forgotten this but Little Kit experiences the ravages of vascular dementia and he has a much better grasp of what madness is than you do.

So what has all this got to do with the matter of Kit the man finding a box in his shed with the bright red shrunken head of John the Baptist inside? Well, the first thing to say is that it all seems a bit implausible. Firstly, there is no reason to suppose that there actually was a box there at all. You know what Little Kit is like; he does sometimes think and believe the oddest things. Then why does he think that the head belonged to John the Baptist, perhaps it was just some other random sort of head that happened to be around. We have seen that human history is a pretty savage sort of affair, and continues to be so. Surely there are all sorts of other people who have had their heads removed. Just because Little Kit says it belongs to the rest of the body of John the Baptist does not mean that this is absolutely true. Yes there is certainly some room four significant doubt there, after all, who would be stupid enough to take the word of a small black and white cat that has never even been to school?

Then there is the question as to why was it shrunken. Surely the head of John the Baptist would be a bit too precious a commodity to muck around with and shrink. If any normal person owned the relic then they would surely protect it rather than try and make it smaller. It just makes no sense.

And then there is the matter of it being red. Surely there can be no reasonable explanation as to why a shrunken head should have turned red.

Well it is a complex turn of events that is for sure! Little Kit has tried in his best detective manner to explain to you what he knows to have happened and yet here you are, still asking questions. Well that is human nature, and is just the way things ought to be, we are all victims of who we are and of our past and our destiny.

So what actually is a cabbage? Of course the correct answer is that a cabbage, as you understand it, probably does not exist at all! As with everything else, if you want to have the truth of anything made real then you will probably need to dig a little bit deeper.

As it happens Little Kit was sitting under an olive tree by a cave on a hill at Gebel Qussqam. He was on an astral travel as he had decided to undertake a pilgrimage to the key points of the flight of the Holy family from Bethlehem southwards. He had called into quite a few places that he used to know well from the times he had accompanied Pharouk and was pleased to see the small garden in Egypt was still there, even though all the vegetables were now different varieties. He visited the area where they used to produce fine resins and he could still feel the presence of the bottle trees and frankincense and dragon-blood and myrrh fading away in the dry brown dustiness of the garden.

The rough tomb where Pharouk's mummified body had been laid to rest was now covered by the perimeter wall of some military installation. He had brought so much prosperity and prestige to the town in his day. Yet due to his disfigured face and quiet disposition he was never much liked by the locals and had been soon forgotten. Kit hoped that his particular boat was happily floating its way through into the afterlife that he had believed in.

The weather was now very hot indeed. When Kit visited Egypt in his astral travels he usually tried to go in the evening, but on this particular day he had made an exception. From his lofty perch he had been able to observe the monks in a nearby monastery shuffling around undertaking their pointless routines.

He was reflecting that it had been a strange old investigation so far. He had been following the "Path of Melancholia" and was now beginning to regret that decision. It had seemed the obvious choice at the start and had helped develop some key aspects of the mystery of the old box that contains the shrunken head of John the Baptist. But it had been a pathway that presented a few too many red herrings and near misses. It was clear that all these connections to particles and protons and physiology and parasites and pirates and philosophy and pheromones was all playing a part, but it was not making a clear view in his mind to explain why Kit the man had found this holy relic seemingly abandoned in a shed in the bottom of a scruffy little garden in a suburb of Cardiff in South Wales.

He decided to look at all the evidence from a different perspective and suddenly all the pieces fell together. Well you have read the book and all the clues are there, can you see why the box is now in the unexpected place it finds itself in.

The answer was revealed to Little Kit when he decided to think a little bit more about all of the people he had investigated who had actually taken possession of the ownership of the box. There was something that that Douggie Hiscox and Daniel Mendoza and Samuel Pallache and Juan Ponce de Leon and all the Mediterranean alchemists and even Philip who had commissioned the box all had in common. In their own peculiar ways they could all be classified as being "reissuance men". All of them were able to say they had a really broad range of interests and expertise. The same was true for those who had a more peripheral involvement.

It was suddenly very clear to Little Kit that he had witnessed the evidence for one of those invisible powers that were beyond human knowledge. It was like the trail of pheromones that the ants leave for others to follow. Quite simply it was the power of the Holy Spirit in the box that had attracted the men to the box. They did not own the box with the head of John the Baptist, the box with the head of John the Baptist owned them,

The reason the box was in the shed at the bottom of the garden was not a matter of some random range of arrangements. The reason the box was concealed in the shed is because that is exactly where the Holy Spirit wanted to be. It had used its strange form of magnetism or inexplicable force to influence the various men it had sought out in order to promote its purpose. The box was at the bottom of the garden at this particular point in time because of some deeper purpose that could not be defined. The box was where it was simply because the Holy Spirit had wanted to come across to South Wales in order to meet Little Kt. Well it was quite flattering really.

Little Kit felt warmly contented with his investigation and revelation, and floated gently back home on his astral plane in order to say a proper hello to the third of the Almighty that had decided to pop over for a visit. Well, it would just be impolite to keep him waiting any longer.

Oh yes, you will have realised that Kit had attended the birthday party of Herod whilst sharing the spirit of the guard Alabast. He had hoped it would just be a good night out. Instead it had all turned out a bit unpleasant and he thought it might end up being one of the worst decisions he had ever made in all his millions of lives. He always felt a bit melancholic whenever he was reminded of it.

.

THE END